THE BEGGARS' BIBLE

THE BEGGARS' BIBLE

By

Louise A. Vernon

Illustrated
by
Jeanie McCoy

HERALD PRESS
Scottdale, Pennsylvania
Waterloo, Ontario

THE BEGGARS' BIBLE
Copyright © 1971 by Herald Press, Scottdale, Pa. 15683
    Published simultaneously in Canada by Herald Press,
    Waterloo, Ont. N2L 6H7. All rights reserved
Library of Congress Catalog Card Number: 77-131534
International Standard Book Number: 0-8361-1732-8
Printed in the United States of America
06 05 04 03 02 01 33 32 31 30 29
65,000 copies in print

To order or request information, please call
1-800-759-4447 (individuals); 1-800-245-7894 (trade).
Website: www.mph.org

Contents

Unwelcome Choice 1

Thirteen-year-old Arnold Hutton hurried to church ahead of his parents. If only he could talk to the preacher, John Wycliffe, before the service began!

"He could tell me what to do," Arnold told himself. "I have to make a choice. I just *have* to."

But he was too late to talk to John Wycliffe before church. Already townspeople and fieldworkers crowded the tiny churchyard, eager to hear the famous Oxford teacher-preacher.

"He's preaching from the gospel," people told each other.

"And a bold, brave man he is for doing so." An old peasant woman thumped her cane on the cobblestones in excitement. "He says a sermon on the gospel should be preached every week in every church in England. God's grace is free."

"Free?" a young man echoed in disbelief. "Then why, after we pay the tithe we owe God, does the church ask for more and more money and goods to buy God's protection? You never hear about God's free grace when those church beggars come around."

"You mustn't talk that way about the friars," an old man said in a shocked voice.

"If a friar isn't a beggar, what is he?" the young man demanded.

"He's a — well, he's a — " Puzzled, the old man scratched his head.

"The word *friar* means *brother*," Arnold volunteered. "He's a brother of the church."

Everyone stared at him, and Arnold bit his lip. Why had he tried to show off his knowledge? He knew everyone expected him to become a friar. *But that's not my choice*, Arnold thought. If he could only talk to John Wycliffe about his dream of going to Oxford University!

When the churchgoers jostled their way toward the church door, Arnold stepped back and let those of higher rank go ahead. As always, he bristled with resentment at the familiar humiliation. If God's grace was free, as John Wycliffe always said, why weren't people free? Why did God allow some men to own whole families, as if they were cows or pigs? Serfs were the lowest, like slaves. Bound men had to stay on their owner's land, but at least bound men — or bondmen, as they were called — could earn money.

Arnold heard someone mention his name. He winced. People had never ceased talking about his being educated with fourteen-year-old Timothy Coombe, son of Sir Malcolm, the owner of the estate where the Huttons and other bondmen lived in thatched-roof cottages.

"Is that the boy you mean? The sturdy one with brown hair?" he heard a visitor ask. "But he looks like a serf."

Arnold tried to move out of earshot and almost ran into the overseer of Sir Malcolm's estate, a clean-shaven man with surly face and hair plastered in peaks over his forehead. The overseer elbowed his way to the visitor.

"I am Sir Malcolm's reeve," he said, "and I can

8

tell you something about this boy you're talking about. He's a serf, all right."

Arnold gritted his teeth in sudden fury. Everyone in Lutterworth knew by this time that Father was a bondman, not a serf any longer. The reeve's dislike of the Hutton family worried Arnold, but he dared not complain. The reeve might ask Father for more tax money.

"Only gentlemen's sons should go to Oxford University," the visitor said. "What kind of future does Sir Malcolm want for this boy?"

Arnold stared at the ground. That was the very question he wanted to discuss with John Wycliffe. If only he could go to college, like Timothy! But college cost money. How could a bondman's son earn enough money to go? Of course, there were two other choices for his future, but Arnold did not want to think about them.

He heard the reeve's malicious chuckle. "Educating the son of a serf is the biggest mistake Sir Malcolm ever made. That boy came from the fields and he'll return to the fields."

Never, Arnold vowed, more than ever distrusting the reeve with his one-sided smile, forever collecting taxes and recording them in his big account book. As overseer for Sir Malcolm, the reeve was hardly better than a bondman himself. How had he managed to buy the fine, fat horse he rode weekdays?

"Why doesn't the boy become a friar?" the visitor suggested.

Arnold shivered in distaste. Could he go around the countryside as a begging brother of the church, coaxing food and hard-earned money from poor people, all the time rolling his eyes heavenward and saying it was all for God? *Never.*

As if in answer to his thoughts, two friars in long, full robes, entered the churchyard, their plump faces wreathed in smiles. When they bobbed their heads in greeting, each showed a round, shaven spot that glistened in the sunshine. One held out a pouch at the end of a long stick. The other cajoled the crowd and gestured toward the pouch. "Put your pennies in here."

"But my penny is for the church collection," someone objected.

"It's all the same. Everything is for the glory of God," the priest intoned.

The people held back, and the friars became more insistent. "God does not bless a grudging giver."

Reluctantly, the churchgoers put their collection pennies into the pouch. The friars beamed, blessed the children, and told them an exciting story about a miser who was carried off by the devil.

Above the murmur and bustle an indignant voice rang out. "What! Begging again?" A frail, stoop-shouldered man in a long black gown with a cord at his waist thrust his way to the friars. His eyes sparked anger above his prominent nose and full, flowing beard.

"Who is this man?" one of the friars asked.

"Ssssh! That is John Wycliffe," people responded from all sides.

The friars glanced at each other under lowered eyelids. "But, Sir John," one protested, emphasizing the courtesy title of *Sir*, by which all preachers were addressed, "Christ Himself was a beggar."

10

John Wycliffe's lips tightened in scorn. "What a notion you friars have gotten — that Christ was a common beggar and His disciples also. Christ was poor and needy and lived a life of poverty, but He never begged from town to town and from house to house with open crying. You friars would rather beg for a poor man's penny than bring a soul from hell."

"Sir John, you should not reprove us like that," one of the friars growled.

"Christ did not let His love for Peter prevent Him from reproving Peter sharply. Why may not men do so to friars, if they trespass more openly and to more harm of Christ's church?"

The church bell rang, and the friars hurried away. Everyone filed into church. Arnold found his parents and sat with them in the back. Perhaps he could talk to John Wycliffe afterward.

As usual, a few people twisted in their seats to stare at Arnold, the one chosen above their own children to be educated. Arnold clenched his fists in silent rebellion. He did not belong to either group, high or low.

Lost in gloomy thought, he watched Sir Malcolm's wife, Lady Edith, flutter in with a servant bringing five-year-old Chad, a spoiled child, who twisted and turned at every step. Then Timothy, Sir Malcolm's fourteen-year-old son, hobbled down the church aisle. Every face turned toward him. Timothy had hurt his leg rescuing his willful young brother from a charging bull. The villagers had talked about the incident for days.

Arnold glanced at Timothy's calm face with its crown of blond hair and felt relieved. The unspoken friendship between them always made everything brighter, even the future.

"Where is Sir Malcolm?" someone whispered.

"Still in London. You know the king is very ill."

A latecomer squeezed in at the back of the church. The fat abbot from the nearby monastery sat down with a grunt and folded his arms across his ample chest. Arnold knew he should feel respect for this man of the church, but he could not. The abbot was a round man with a round haircut. A girdle encircled his round middle. Even his fingers were blunted at the ends. What had fattened a man who had taken vows to serve only God?

Arnold stifled a sigh. After church the abbot would try as usual to coax him to enter the monastery by saying God wanted him to. *Why would God tell the abbot and not me?* he asked himself.

John Wycliffe began his sermon with an apology for his display of temper. "Christian men should beware in their speech against friars," he said, "for some are good. But if they are evil, men should point out this evil. Christian men should know pseudo-friars and what is good in their order and what is evil. Much of their order is good, as is said in God's law, but much is evil and is in discord with God's law. The church teaches one thing and friars do another."

As he talked, Wycliffe's voice became more vehement. "Begging friars are like turtles. They find their way, one after the other, through the whole country. They penetrate every house, like lap dogs of ladies of rank. What sums of money are spent on them and how little on the education of children."

12

At these words, Arnold jerked his head straight up. Here was a clue to the mystery of his education. John Wycliffe had taught Sir Malcolm at Oxford years before. Was there a connection between Sir Malcolm's decision to educate a poor boy and Wycliffe's views?

After the sermon, the abbot cornered John Wycliffe in the churchyard. "Why are you stirring up the people against friars?"

"Since friars sin often, why shouldn't men reprove them in their beard, but ever by meekness and love? Woe be unto us if we keep still and speak not against their sins, when we know they sin openly and many souls after them just as Satan does," Wycliffe retorted.

The thunder this frail man put into his words astonished Arnold. Where did he get such power?

"When a person is ordered to give of his goods more than God Himself demands through His law, then that person should not give these goods," Wycliffe continued. "It is as much of a sin to rob a widow or a poor, fatherless child of a penny or a halfpenny as it is to rob a rich man of a hundred marks' worth of goods."

The abbot flushed with anger. "Sir John, you are going too far. Your influential friends at court are not going to bear with your views forever, and the church will not let itself be dishonored."

"Does God listen to prelates and friars more than others on account of their red cheeks and fat lips?"

Arnold listened in amazement and delight. He longed to be as daring and outspoken as John Wycliffe, to fight evil and wrongdoing with such courage.

Wycliffe's voice rose. "No word of Christ's justifies

13

the mendicant orders except one: 'I know you not' "
(Matthew 25:12).

Arnold remembered those words months later in
connection with Sir Malcolm's five-year-old son.
Arnold was waiting as usual at the private chapel
near the manor house for the priest, and as usual he
braced himself for the daily taunts of little Chad. The
boy pranced back and forth on a red stick horse, his
blond hair bobbing under a blue cap.

"You're nothing but — you're nothing but — you're
nothing but a *serf*," Chad sang out.

Arnold flinched. The humiliating word *serf* hurt.
Would there always be someone like Chad to remind
him of his low rank? Arnold wanted to strike out, hit
back, hurt someone to relieve his pain, but of course
he could not hit a nobleman's son.

He forced himself to stand rigid and to gaze with
seeming indifference over Chad's head past the open
double gates to the fields beyond, where Sir Malcolm's
serfs and bondmen harvested grain. The reeve came
through the gate hugging his big account book to his
chest. He crossed the courtyard to the house in his
usual way, close to the wall, to avoid his shadow.

"Why have you come to the chapel?" he asked
Arnold in mock surprise. "You belong out in the
fields. Once a serf, always a serf."

Anger blazed up in Arnold, but he held his temper. Was he to end up in the fields, as the reeve
said? Or would he have to enter the monastery across
from the thatched-roof cottages at the far end of the
field, become fat like the abbot in his billowing robes,
and wheedle people out of their money, claiming it
was for the glory of God?

Chad galloped closer. "Serf! Serf!" he called in malicious glee.

The hated word bounced around the courtyard walls. *But Father was a bondman, now*. Ever since he had broken his leg and Mother had taught him to sew, Father had amazed Sir Malcolm's household with his deftness in using a needle. As a bondman tailor, Father earned more than fieldworkers. If only he could buy his freedom! Never again would Arnold be forced to listen to insults like Chad's.

On a reckless impulse, Chad rushed up and flicked Arnold with a toy whip. "On your knees! You're a beggar. I'll give you alms."

A *beggar*, Arnold raged to himself. That was the worst insult yet. On market days at Lutterworth, he had stared with loathing at the whining, miserable creatures in their rags, hardly worse than the begging friars who coaxed people to give up hoarded coins or precious food. "For the love of God," the beggars and friars always said. What a strange phrase! Did God love people in return?

These thoughts reminded Arnold of the two choices for his future — the monastery or the fields.

Chad was stamping his foot in fury. "Get down on your knees. You're a beggar."

"I won't be a beggar. My father is a bondman."

"Just another name for serf," Chad retorted.

Arnold clenched his fists. Chad retreated on his stick horse to a safe distance. "All right. You're not a serf," he called. "You're a slave, and when you grow up, all your children will be slaves, forever and ever."

Goaded beyond endurance, Arnold seized a clod of dirt and flung it at the small boy's mocking face. The dirt crumbled in Chad's open mouth. He clawed at it, howled in terror, and headed for the manor house.

"Timothy! Timothy!" he screamed.

Arnold slumped against the chapel door. Now he was in trouble. A bondman's son hitting a nobleman's child! Why hadn't he controlled his temper? Then he remembered how John Wycliffe had lost his temper with the friars and the abbot. But Wycliffe had a good reason.

Chad's brother Timothy limped out of the house. The sight of Timothy melted Arnold's anger. He would not have spoiled the secret friendship between them for anything.

"Don't be so noisy, Chad. What's the matter?"

Timothy's calm voice soothed Arnold. Timothy deserved to be a nobleman's son. Thoughtful, fair-minded, and polite, Timothy had never mentioned Arnold's low rank in all the years they had studied together.

"He hit me! He hit me!" Chad blubbered. "He has no right to. He's nothing but a — "

Timothy steered Chad toward the house. "Go inside and have someone clean you up."

Chad scampered away. Arnold hung his head and waited for Timothy to scold him.

"Chad hasn't learned any better," Timothy said in his usual measured tones. "He's got big ears. The reeve has been complaining about the poor crops because there aren't enough men to work in the fields. Every time he sees your father sewing for my mother, he takes it as a personal insult, and then, of course, it doesn't help when he sees you come here every day for school."

"Your own father ordered me to," Arnold reminded Timothy in a muffled voice.

"I know. I know. Did I ever tell you how it all started? John Wycliffe wanted to prove to my father that a serf could learn as much as anyone."

Arnold breathed easily again. So that was why he was being educated! Somehow, the word *serf* lost its sting. He was glad he had studied hard.

"And I must say," Timothy added, "you've really proved yourself. You're as ready for Oxford as I am, even if you are only thirteen. The priest told me so himself." Timothy looked around. "He's late today. He must be with Mother. I'll go find him." He limped off.

Arnold wanted to run after him, to tell Timothy how much he longed to go to Oxford, but how could he without seeming to beg for help? Begging was something he would never do.

Chad galloped out of the house, his face clean and shining with impudence. "You're just a slave," he told Arnold. "The reeve says so. I'm a nobleman's son, and you have to do what I say. We're going to play beggars, so get down on your knees."

"No, I won't."

Chad sulked. "My father's home from London. I'm going to tell him you hit me, and do you know what'll happen then?"

Arnold seethed with fresh resentment. He knew well enough. He would be sent to the fields, yet if he knelt like a beggar, even in play, he would betray something in himself. He groaned inwardly. No matter what he chose, he would be the loser. What possible choice could he make?

A Difficult Lesson

2

Chad's expression of haughty triumph was too much for Arnold.

"No, I won't play beggars."

Chad started off at a run and met Timothy coming out of the manor house. "I'm going to tell Father," he said loud enough for Arnold to overhear.

"Tell Father what?" Timothy asked.

"He won't play beggars with me, and I'm going to tell Father he hit me, and Father'll send him out to the fields. The reeve said so."

The reeve again, Arnold thought. *Was that where Chad received his ideas of superiority?*

Timothy flushed in annoyance. "Don't be so willful, Chad. It will get you into trouble one day. Remember the bull."

Backed by Timothy's unspoken support, Arnold choked down his pride and knelt. "I'm kneeling, Chad." Perhaps this act of humiliation would be sufficient punishment for losing his temper. He hoped so. After all, people had been put in the stocks for less offense.

Chad, uncertain, cupped his fingers over Arnold's head. "Now beg," he said in a small voice.

Arnold knew the little boy was remembering how his adored older brother had been hurt rescuing him from the bull.

18

Men's voices sounded nearby. Sir Malcolm, pale from Parliament sessions in London, was showing a visitor around the estate. With a start, Arnold recognized the slight, stoop-shouldered John Wycliffe. The rector glanced at the boys; his lips turned down in disapproval.

"Sir Malcolm, I do not like to see human subjection, even in play."

"Chad, stop that," Sir Malcolm ordered and waited until Arnold rose.

"It reminds me, however, that we must never rest until England is rid of slavery," Wycliffe continued.

Sir Malcolm's shaggy eyebrows rose in astonishment. "There hasn't been a slave in England since 1324. That's fifty-two years."

The two men walked on, their voices rising in a heated discussion.

Chad watched, his blue eyes round in fascination. "What makes Sir John holler like that?"

"Not so loud, Chad," Timothy cautioned. "He might hear you. Sir John is always fighting for a cause."

"But why is he so angry with Father?"

"It isn't anger. He just gets excited about ideas."

The boys watched Sir Malcolm face the rector. "You and your quick temper have just about ruined me, Sir John."

Wycliffe looked surprised and penitent. "I confess I too readily impart a sinister, vindictive zeal into a line of argument. Some have called it hypocrisy, hatred, and rancor under a pretense of holiness. I fear — and I admit it with sorrow — that this has happened to me too frequently. I confess my sin sorrowing, but I ask God for grace. But how have these personal faults hurt you?"

"You and your continual criticism of the friars! The good abbot was so insulted he may not buy my land, and if he doesn't, I can't pay my taxes this year."

"The abbot and others like him probably would not pay the value of the land, anyway," Wycliffe said. "These little antichrists rob men of their goods, claim it is for spiritual things, and then keep much of this muck for themselves. They eat up what would keep many families, and four or five needy men might be clothed in one cape and hood of your worthy neighbor, the abbot. As for monks and friars, many love the cloth of their habit more than the cloth of charity."

Arnold could see that John Wycliffe was ready to talk on and on, but Sir Malcolm interrupted.

"All this may be very true, but I have my taxes to pay. The abbot has made me a good offer."

"Have you no faith in God?" Wycliffe asked.

"What is faith?" Sir Malcolm snorted.

"Faith is to believe what you do not see," Wycliffe answered.

"Faith won't pay my debts. I tell you, the land must go."

"What about your bondmen?" Wycliffe asked.

"They'll belong to the monastery. They go with the land. You know that."

"That is slavery," Wycliffe responded with spirit. "Selling into slavery is not God's law."

"The bondmen will stay in their cottages and till the same soil. What difference does it make to them whether they work for me or for the abbot?"

"It means the abbot's belly gets fatter and his cheeks redder."

"Now, Sir John, I know you don't like prelates, monks, and friars, but don't start in on that again. As for preaching sermons on the gospel to lay people — " Sir Malcolm shuddered. "How can they be expected to understand a theologian trained at Oxford University? They have their country priests, their penny for the church collection. Let that do."

"It is not enough," Wycliffe said. "They need Scripture."

Sir Malcolm's mouth dropped open. "I hope the Pope never finds out what you've been saying lately. He'd send a fleet of Rome runners to Bishop Courtenay forbidding you to speak or write."

John Wycliffe smiled. "Sharp words bite often where soft speech does not move. Scripture is God's law, and I shall never stop saying so. All Christians ought to know Holy Writ and to defend it."

Sir Malcolm gestured in impatience. "You know, Sir John, your ideas are becoming more radical every year. You must watch your words. We don't want you labeled as a heretic, you know, especially since you're my friend. Now, no more of this. My private priest said he wanted to talk to me today, probably about the boys. He should be here by now to teach them. I must admit that little serf you insisted on educating has done very well."

Arnold grinned at Timothy and watched the manor house priest approach with his head lowered and his hands hidden under the folds of his long robe. The priest glanced up, saw John Wycliffe, and with an expression of horror, turned as if to run.

"What is the matter with you?" Sir Malcolm demanded. "Why did you want to speak to me?"

The priest gulped. "Sir Malcolm, I have come to tell you I must leave."

"Leave? For what reason? Don't I pay you your stipend?"

"Yes, truly, sir."

"Don't I feed you well?"

"Yes, truly, sir."

"Then what is your complaint?"

The priest jerked his head toward John Wycliffe. "My superiors have ordered me not to live so near a man who works for Satan."

At these words, John Wycliffe's lips curled upward in a smile. Then he frowned, but said nothing.

"What nonsense is this?" Sir Malcolm demanded. "Who will return grace at table? Who will pray for our souls? Who will teach the boys?"

"I am sure you will find someone," the priest said, "but if you have any regard for the welfare of their souls, you will remove them from Satan's disciple." He bowed and left.

Sir Malcolm paced in front of John Wycliffe. "Now, Sir John, you must have been saying some pretty sharp things down there at Oxford to bring on such an accusation. Why can't you keep your ideas to yourself, preach and teach according to church tradition, and stay friendly with the friars the way you used to? Do you want all four groups to fight you?" He did not wait for an answer. "What am I to do about Timothy entering Oxford this fall?"

"I'll prepare him myself," John Wycliffe said. "Let him come to me tomorrow."

22

Arnold tried not to show his dismay. Was he to choose between field and monastery so soon?

"Send both boys," Wycliffe added.

The next day at Lutterworth Church, William Newbold, the parish priest, asked the boys to wait outside Wycliffe's study until the rector was through speaking to a group of Oxford students. In a little while, a few of the students came out talking with high-pitched enthusiasm.

"You don't do it with words," one said. "Sir John says we would never do any open begging from house to house."

"How would we live, then?" another asked.

Arnold puzzled over the strange conversation. Why would rich Oxford students be interested in begging? He listened to other students.

"What did Sir John say about the Pope?" a student asked.

Another laughed. "He said the Pope was antichrist enclosed in a castle."

"And that he was poison under the color of holiness," a third student chimed in.

"Don't forget he called the Pope Christ's enemy," still another student added.

Others chuckled over Wycliffe's calling friars foul worms' meat.

One student was critical. "I've heard all Wycliffe's doings are to one end — to spread his words, his fame, and opinion among men."

Later, when the last student had left, and Arnold and Timothy were in John Wycliffe's study, Arnold repeated the student's remark. Wycliffe leaned back in his carved chair and put his fingertips together.

"The Lord, by His power and grace opened my mind to understand the Scriptures, but often for vainglory I departed from the teaching of them. My double aim was to acquire dazzling fame among the people and lay bare the pride of the sophists."

Why would Wycliffe make such a confession? Arnold asked himself. The answer came after a few weeks of Wycliffe's tutoring. The rector announced both boys were ready to matriculate at Oxford.

"What good will that do me?" Arnold burst out. "I can never go to college. I'm only a — "

Wycliffe checked the rush of words with a wave of his hand. "Flee pride and you will conquer Satan."

Arnold marveled at Wycliffe's humility in confessing his own shortcomings.

"Should I enter a monastery?" Arnold asked.

"Perpetual vows are unlawful," Wycliffe replied. "Many have made men religious against their will. Christ Himself cannot compel anyone to enter religion. You can be what God intends, but you must make His will your choice. Study His Son's patience."

Make His will your choice. The words echoed in Arnold's ears all the way home. How could a person know he was choosing what God willed?

At the cottage he could see his father talking to the plump abbot near the gate of the walled-in monastery. Mother came to the doorway. "I hope this is the last day Sir Malcolm permits your father to sew for the abbot. Lady Edith wants him to finish Timothy's clothes before he goes to Oxford."

There it was again. Timothy would soon go on to college. What was left for Arnold? The fields or the monastery? Which was God's will?

"Sir John says I am ready for Oxford, Mother, but what is the use thinking about it?"

Mother was silent for a moment. "You can enter the monastery and continue your studies there. The abbot has promised us you could."

"But I don't want to live like that," Arnold burst out. "To be a monk and never leave the monastery, or become a friar and go around begging for money — oh, Mother, why are some people rich and some poor? Why did God make them that way?"

"God works His will in strange ways sometimes," Mother admitted. "Your father was once a serf, and because he broke his leg he is now a bondman."

"But that was because he learned how to be a tailor. That doesn't help me. How can I go to Oxford University?"

"I've heard that many students beg their way from one day to the next."

"Mother!" All of Arnold's pent-up indignation exploded. "Do you want me to become a common beggar?"

Begging again. Could he ever escape being reminded of his low rank? Should he go to Oxford and beg on the streets for crumbs of learning? Arnold shrank from the idea. That surely was not God's will. But what had John Wycliffe said? It was every person's obligation to find out what God intended for him, and then choose to do it. A natural curiosity and hope awakened in Arnold. He waited for Father to finish talking to the abbot to tell him about Wycliffe's ideas, but Father and the abbot kept on with their discussion too far away for Arnold to hear a word.

Jock, the manor estate clown, trudged past the

cottage with another bondman, their gleanings from the early fall harvest in sacks across their shoulders. Jock jerked his head in the direction of Father and the abbot.

"I hope for your sake the abbot isn't coming to eat supper with you," he told Mother. "With his appetite he could eat half a winter's food. Besides, you'd have to feed his dogs a loaf and find a hen for his hawk." Jock chuckled wryly. "I understand at the monastery the hunting dogs outnumber the monks two to one."

"You mustn't say such disrespectful things," Mother chided, but she hid a smile.

Jock grinned at Arnold. "I hear your teacher is our good rector himself. I remember years ago when Sir John was visiting here, long before he became rector at Lutterworth, he was arguing with Sir Malcolm; said he could take any boy, even the son of a serf, and educate him. Sir Malcolm said it was impossible. And then you toddled out into the road, a mere slip of a lad with your big brown eyes and laughed up at him. That started it all."

Arnold stifled a sigh. He couldn't laugh now — not when he would soon have to choose his future.

The bondmen shifted their sacks and headed toward their thatched-roof cottages. Father left the abbot and came home, his face cheerful.

It must be about me, Arnold decided. Had Father and the abbot arranged for him to enter the monastery? Was that what God intended?

Jock, the estate clown, chuckled wryly. "I understand at the
monastery the hunting dogs outnumber
the monks two to one."

Court Decision 3

Father did not mention his talk with the abbot, and Arnold did not ask, in hopes of putting off the dreaded moment of deciding his future. He longed to confess to his parents about hitting Chad, but could not bring himself to talk about the painful incident. He hoped the whole thing would be forgotten, but his guilty secret hung like a millstone around his neck.

At dawn a few days later, the dull scrape of a knife against stone woke him. Astonished at the unusual sound so early in the day, he pushed aside the coverlet on his sack of straw, leaned on one elbow, and listened. The ground underneath the thin layer of rushes hurt his arm. He wriggled to a sitting position, hugged his knees, and listened to the scraping. As light came through the tiny latticed window, he saw his father lift up a square stone from the hearth in the middle of the room. Mother bent down and tugged at a dirt-covered, brown leather pouch until it pulled free.

She clucked in dismay and brushed at the dirt. " 'Tis a pity to spoil good leather."

"Never mind the dirt," Father chuckled. "It's what is inside that counts, as our good rector keeps telling us."

Arnold heard the clink of metal. "It's money," he thought in amazement. Where would Father get so much money? There must be more than the begging friars gathered on their rounds.

Father opened the pouch, poured a pile of coins on the roughhewn table, and counted the money into neat piles.

"Twenty-six pounds, thirteen shillings, and eight pence," he announced.

"Is it enough?"

Arnold's hopes soared. Had they saved the money to send him to Oxford University?

Father brought out a handful of white tally sticks and laid them on the table. "It is now."

"What are those?" Mother asked.

"The abbot paid me for the tailoring I did."

"*Paid* you? Why, those sticks aren't money."

"The abbot said they are as good as money."

Mother seemed satisfied. "So this is the working of God's law that Sir John is always talking about. Who would have thought a broken leg would have led to your buying your freedom?"

Arnold listened in embarrassment. How could he have been so selfish as to think this money would send him to Oxford University? Father's freedom was far better. Then a sudden suspicion darted into his mind. What if Father had stolen money from the manor house? Maybe the reeve left money around to tempt Father, or even left the white tally sticks out. None of Sir Malcolm's bondmen liked the reeve, whose secretive airs and fat horse roused suspicion about his honesty.

Arnold could hold back no longer. "Father, where did you get all that money?"

Father laughed. "I didn't steal it. This money has

been honestly earned, and it means freedom for us. No more will we Huttons be slaves, serfs, villeins, bondmen. We'll be free men of England. Arnold, your children and their children, forever and ever, will be free."

"Free!" Arnold echoed. Then the whole family could go to the city of Oxford. Somehow, someway, he could go to one of the Oxford colleges. The sudden hope made him dizzy. Surely, this was God's plan for him.

Later, the reeve came to the cottage, opened his account book, and checked off their names. "Sir Malcolm is holding manor court tomorrow. Everyone must be there." The reeve spoke as if he were a long way off. Arnold sensed his annoyance at having to do the work belonging to the beadle.

"But this is such short notice," Father protested.

The reeve made a reluctant explanation. "John Wycliffe has been summoned to appear before the king's council, and Sir Malcolm is going to London with him."

"Then tomorrow I buy my freedom from Sir Malcolm," Father announced.

"What!" The reeve jumped back. His face worked in surprise. "You mean you have enough money?"

"Yes, with the white tally sticks you gave me," Father said with pride.

"The white tally sticks?" Again the reeve's face worked. "Very well, I'll take the money."

"I'd like to give it to Sir Malcolm myself," Father said.

"But you can't buy your freedom directly," the reeve explained. "Actually, in a court of law you are still a serf, and a serf cannot own anything; therefore he cannot buy anything. You will have to deal with me as a third party."

Father turned over the money with reluctance. As the reeve passed Arnold on his way out, he spoke in an undertone. "I haven't forgotten about you. Tomorrow at court you will get the punishment you deserve."

Anger and concern unsettled Arnold for the rest of the day. What would the punishment be? Would Sir Malcolm order him to be put in the stocks, with his feet and hands dangling? Or would he be whipped in front of everyone?

The next day Sir Malcolm's bondmen and their families gathered under the oak tree talking at fever pitch. Sir Malcolm was going to sell his land to the abbot, and that meant the bondmen would be working for the abbot as their overlord. A chorus of voices sounded the general discontent.

"It's the times," someone explained. "Sir Malcolm can't pay his taxes. England has never been the same since the Black Death."

When the bondmen learned that Father was going to buy his freedom that very day, their complaints turned to congratulations.

"Aye, seemly it is," an old man proclaimed, "that one of us can buy his freedom. If one can, we all can."

"Aye, aye," the others shouted.

"That you can indeed," Father said, "if you work hard and save your money. No more quaffing ale by the tankard."

"Aye, aye."

"Jock here saves his money down his gullet," someone put in slyly. "He's saved enough to buy freedom for us all."

"I have to buy food for three little ones," Jock spluttered. "You have only one," he told Father. "What good is freedom for this lad? He'll be in the monastery anyway."

Everyone takes it for granted, Arnold thought.

The abbot appeared at the gate on a magnificent horse. He dismounted and motioned to two mendicant friars walking behind him. They immediately mingled with the crowd and hurried to make the rounds selling pardons and pins. They joked and told stories, but today the money did not flow as usual into their pouches.

One of the friars held up a ragged square of cloth. "This is from the robe of the Venerable Bede, one of England's first Christians," he said. "How much?"

The friar, almost as plump as the abbot who looked gloomily on, beamed at the onlookers. The people drew back.

"Sir Malcolm has not yet paid us for the grain," a bondman explained.

"We do not have our share yet of oats," another added.

"Remember to pay your tithes first," the friar warned.

"How can anyone tithe one egg?" Jock drawled.

At the laughter, the friars looked annoyed and soon left, their pouches almost as flat as before. Almost on their heels two young barefoot friars joined the group. Unlike other begging friars, these were clad in russet gowns as red as apples. Their big patch pockets were empty. Each friar had a walking stick, but neither pouches nor gloves for handling money.

"There seems to be an air of celebration," one said in a pleasant, cultivated voice. Arnold tried to remember where he had heard a voice like that before.

"Yes. Good man here is buying his freedom," someone said.

"Indeed, this is cause for rejoicing. 'To every thing there is a season, and a time to every purpose under the heaven.' "

"What strange words these are," people murmured.

"They're from Scripture," one of the young men explained.

"What's Scripture?" a child asked.

"God's Word."

The abbot made a strange, gurgling sound and edged closer. One of the young men began a story. "Once there was a man who sold all his land — "

"Just like Sir Malcolm," Jock blurted. "He's going to sell his land to the monastery so he can pay his taxes."

"But the man I am telling you about sold his land because he found something of great price that money couldn't buy."

The abbot cleared his throat and stepped up to the two young men. "Who are you?"

"Call us 'Poor Priests.' "

"You are neither Augustinians, Franciscans, Carmelites, or Dominicans. None of the four orders has friars who wear this garb."

"We are just Poor Priests," the young man said.

The abbot gave an angry tug at his waist cord. "By what authority do you take it on yourselves to tell stories from Scripture?"

"By God's law."

The abbot's face turned purple. He tucked his hands in his long sleeves. "Ah! Is your master by chance the talkative doctor of Oxford?"

"John Wycliffe has prepared us. We are Oxford students."

Then Arnold remembered the group at John Wycliffe's study in Lutterworth.

"You have no right to beg," the abbot thundered. "You mock the mendicant friars by taking money from the poor and using it for yourselves."

The young men laughed. "We do not beg. We have neither scrip nor shoes, no pouches on sticks, and no gloves."

The abbot glowered. "Then how will you live?"

"By what people give us of their own free will."

The abbot's jowls reddened. "Then begone from here. This John Wycliffe is going to have to answer for all the trouble he is causing." The abbot shooed the two russet-clad poor priests out of the courtyard. A few minutes later he came over to Mother and Father. "I hope I have not heard correctly about your son."

Arnold's heart gave a convulsive leap. Did everyone but his parents know he had hit Chad and was going to be punished for it?

"What do you mean?" Father asked.

The abbot's eyes beamed with forced friendliness. "Your son, then, has not been under the corrupt influence of Doctor Wicked-believe?"

"Who?" Mother asked in shocked amazement.

The abbot fingered the tips of the cord around his waist. "I mean to say John Wycliffe, the learned doctor who scuttles from Oxford to — " he nodded in the direction of Lutterworth, "his rectory near the river Swift. Too bad the river is not swift enough to carry him away." A malicious chuckle burst from the abbot's lips. "I would hate to see your very intelligent boy influenced by the doctor's heretical arguments."

At these words, a fierce loyalty to John Wycliffe leaped up in Arnold. The abbot, with his fine clothes, rich food, his hunting dogs and trained falcons, could never understand in a thousand years a man like John Wycliffe, who ate barely enough to keep himself alive and who practiced what he preached. Arnold vowed he would never go to the monastery. *Never.*

The talk among the bond people flowed on.

"You mean Sir Malcolm is selling us to the monastery?" a latecomer asked.

"Why not? It is his right," another answered.

"But ever since the Black Death men have been treated more like men than cattle. Otherwise, they would run away."

Jock, the witty one, flexed his muscles and pretended to be up for auction. "What am I worth?"

"Why, sirrah, three eggs a week and three days' work a month," someone called out.

"Men should not be sold. It is against God's law," another pointed out.

"Where did you hear that?"

"Why, from our good rector, John Wycliffe. We are

all God's children and should live as brethren."

"Then I for one will no more be bond. I will be Christ's man," Jock exclaimed.

"Yes, that you will, when you are sold to the abbot," others laughed.

Sir Malcolm and the reeve took their places at a big table under the oak tree. John Wycliffe, in a long traveling coat, stood nearby.

The reeve opened his book and called a name. A man stepped up.

"You have caused these chattels to be lost to the manor," the reeve said, "one flail cut from holly, one harrow made of ash, one armload of reeds for thatching."

"But, my lord," the man protested to Sir Malcolm, "I needed these to rebuild my cottage."

"Make good this loss," Sir Malcolm decreed. The first court decision of the day had been made. The reeve noted it in his book.

The abbot complained about a bondman who had been loaned to him by Sir Malcolm. "This man owes me money."

"But, my lord," the man exclaimed, "how can I be fined unless I am allowed to earn and hoard money? Besides, my lord, he beat me until I cannot work."

The onlookers murmured disapproval.

"Only fine him hereafter," Sir Malcolm stated.

"But this man owes me a tithe," the abbot protested.

"Exact your tithes by the holiness of your life," John Wycliffe spoke up. "Why should a poor man's money feed a flock of antichrists? Such money does the parish no good nor the general holy church. It's hypocrisy — " He stopped abruptly and walked away, as if he feared his own temper.

Sir Malcolm waited for the next name to be called.

"Not here, my lord," a woman said.

The onlookers craned their necks. Unexcused absences could be fined a day and a half's wages.

Sir Malcolm levied the fine. The woman burst into tears.

The reeve whispered to Sir Malcolm.

"Arnold Hutton," Sir Malcolm called.

Arnold jumped at the sound of his name and made his way to the table.

"The reeve says you hit my son."

The bond people murmured again. "Ungrateful boy. After all Sir Malcolm has done for him," they whispered.

"Is this true?" Sir Malcolm asked.

"Yes, my lord."

"Why did you do it?"

"He called me a serf."

Sir Malcolm drummed his fingers on the table. "Didn't I pluck you from the fields and educate you?"

Arnold nodded, unable to speak.

"Did you know that John Wycliffe persuaded me to have you educated?"

"Yes," Arnold all but whispered.

"How do you think he will feel about this act of yours?"

Arnold was close to tears. "I — I don't know, but I lost my temper, Sir Malcolm."

Sir Malcolm's face softened at the apology. Then, to everyone's amazement, he burst into laughter. "I

The abbot bustled to the court table. "Give the boy to me. Let him expiate his sin by coming to the monastery."

think perhaps he would understand, at that. Sir John has always had a great deal of trouble with his own temper. However, you must make restitution for this act."

The abbot bustled to the court table. "Give the boy to me. Let him expiate his sin — for it *is* a sin — by coming to the monastery and preparing for a career in the church."

"No, no," Arnold gasped.

Sir Malcolm thought for a moment. "Yes, I think this is a good solution." He leaned toward Arnold. "Or would you rather go back to the fields?"

That's no better, Arnold thought. If Sir Malcolm sold his lands to the abbot, Arnold would still be under the abbot's control. He groaned. There was no way out.

Too Much Freedom 4

Arnold consoled himself with one happy thought. At least Mother and Father would be free. When Father's name was called, he came to the table and stood before Sir Malcolm.

"So you want to be a freeman," Sir Malcolm mused. "Well, a squire is not content unless he can live as a knight. The knight wants to be a baron, the baron an earl, and an earl a king."

Father smiled. "True, my lord."

"Have you turned over to the reeve your freedom fee?"

"Yes, my lord."

The reeve interrupted. "My lord, this man gave me no such sum."

"But with the tally sticks —" Father began.

The reeve whispered to Sir Malcolm and pointed to the account book. A murmur swelled like a faraway hum of bees among the bond people.

"The poor man's word is not believed in court," someone whispered.

"No," others agreed. "For the poor man, they do not keep justice."

"This justice is a source of income for certain people," Jock muttered.

Sir Malcolm looked at the reeve, then at Father.

"You say you gave the money to the reeve, and he says you did not give him enough. I have no time to settle that now. Sir John and I must leave for London." He rose. "Since I am selling my land to the abbot, this matter will have to be settled with him." Sir Malcolm dismissed the court.

The bond people poured out their sympathy to Father. Arnold forced back his indignation. How could anyone trust God's law that John Wycliffe always talked about, after such injustice?

With a heavy heart he said good-bye to his parents and started toward the monastery. He and a man with a wooden hoe arrived at the gate at the same time.

"What's the time of day?" the man asked Arnold.

"Past noon," Arnold replied.

The man's bright eyes twinkled. "Are you coming here to stay?"

"I — I may," Arnold admitted. "Do you belong here?"

"I'm one of the abbot's serfs." The man seemed proud of it.

"Oh, that's too bad."

"Why? All I have to do is obey my superiors and I will go to heaven."

"But you are not free."

"How free is anyone? Call me serf, or villein, or bondman, or whatever you want. What's in a name?"

Arnold had not thought of it that way. "You don't sound like a serf."

"Oh, I wasn't born a serf, but I gave myself up to the church as donatio. I went to the abbot and I said, 'You shall give me food and bed and twenty-six shillings a year, and I shall become your man of my body.' "

"Why don't you become a monk?"

"I can't read or write."

"Do monks work in the fields?"

The serf laughed. "In this house, they don't even do their kitchen or housework. The abbot has more servants than brethren. Why, these monks don't garden or mow the cloister garth. You'll see for yourself."

Dreading what was to come, Arnold waited for the gatekeeper to summon a monk. Arnold followed him through hushed halls to the kitchen. The cook, a man with a wide mouth and big stomach, grinned a welcome and put Arnold to work stirring a huge cauldron of porridge.

The next morning the cook shredded freshly baked white bread into a huge bowl of warm milk. Arnold watched in envious silence. If he were a monk, he would be eating this fine food. The delicious aroma made his mouth water.

"Can't the monks break up their own bread?" he asked.

The cook stopped his work, his hands in midair. "The monks? This is for the abbot's puppies."

Arnold could not believe his ears. "Do they get *all* of it?"

The cook grunted in disgust. "That they do. I haven't eaten white bread since Michaelmas last year."

"But why should the abbot's puppies feed better than his men?"

The cook did not seem to hear. "Hurry with this

milk. I hear the puppies yelping. I've never said it around here, but if the abbot paid more attention to God than his dogs, people would pay their tithes more willingly."

Arnold carried the bowl outside to the puppies' enclosure. They gulped milk and bread until their stomachs bulged, then snuggled down to sleep.

The cook hurried out, wiping his hands on his soiled yellow apron. "Make yourself scarce. The abbot has a visitor, the master of the Carmelite friary at Ipswich and two of his friars. They want to buy some puppies. Don't let them see you, or you might find yourself on the road to Ipswich."

"Do you mean the abbot might sell me?" Arnold asked in horror.

The cook snorted. "There's not much honor among thieves. They might steal you."

Arnold scrambled out of sight behind sacks of grain near the door.

"Keep your eyes and ears open and your mouth closed," the cook said. "You'll learn plenty about men of God."

Four men bustled past Arnold to where the puppies slept.

"My dear brother John," the abbot began.

"Don't call me John," the first of the guests said in an aggrieved tone. "Call me Brother Kenningham. This fellow we spoke of is called John, and that unworthily, for he has cast away the grace that God has given him."

"And you must admit, Brother Kenningham, with all his acts in the schools, he has barked against the church," the abbot said. "He has invented many new opinions without any grounds, and the patience of John of Gaunt has been exhausted. John Wycliffe has gone to London even now to answer to the king's council."

"Wycliffe has found favor from the court for twenty years," one of the friars ventured.

"Bishop Courtenay is very displeased, and now that the bishop is in London, I am sure action will be taken. When the good bishop was chancellor at Oxford a few years ago, he was suspicious about Wycliffe's views."

"Even granting that Wycliffe is the foremost scholar in England doesn't excuse his personal vanity in desiring to spread his name and fame among men," Brother Kenningham said.

"But no one can call Wycliffe a hypocrite in his personal life. He lives what he speaks of in principle," one of the friars said.

The abbot frowned at this defense. "His erroneous and heretical conclusions are lying and absurd," he snapped. "Sir John has the twofold privilege of changing his opinions at will and of being right every time." The abbot laughed at his own humor. "The next step is excommunication."

"You know what Wycliffe says about that, do you not?" Brother Kenningham asked. "He says that unjust excommunication would set up the Pope above God and ruin the Christian church."

"Ridiculous!" The abbot pointed out the sleeping puppies. The visitors circled the dogs and discussed them with the same fervor that they had discussed Wycliffe.

Arnold slipped back to the kitchen. Did Wycliffe

know that people were talking about him? Arnold longed to hear more of Wycliffe's views about God and the church. How could the abbot and his guests talk about people with the same enthusiasm as they talked about dogs? Arnold could not imagine John Wycliffe being so concerned.

The cook lifted his eyebrows in an "I-told-you-so" expression, and cocked his head toward the hall. Arnold heard a strange sound — the sound of a small boy crying.

"They're taking them younger and younger," the cook muttered.

Arnold stared at him in shocked understanding. Had the monks stolen a child? Something about the cries sounded familiar. He peered out into the shadowed hall. There was Chad rubbing his eyes with doubled fists.

Two of the visiting friars tried to hush Chad. The abbot hurried in. "Who is making such unseemly sounds? Who is this boy?"

The friars shrugged. "We found him alone on the road to Oxford. We can make a respectable little friar out of him after he learns humility and obedience."

Torn between feelings of sympathy and secret revenge, Arnold watched Chad. The little boy's willfulness had brought real trouble to him. *You deserve what is happening*, he thought.

"Who is he?"

"I don't know. Every time I ask his name, he kicks me in the shins."

Arnold grinned in spite of himself. That sounded like Chad, all right. Then the enormity of what could happen gradually dawned on him. The friars would take Chad with them, back to Ipswich. His father, mother, and Timothy would never be able to see him without a friar being present.

Arnold ducked back into the kitchen. "That's Sir Malcolm's son," he told the cook.

The cook started up. "It truly is? Oh, that means trouble, trouble. Are these men of God picking up children instead of hunting dogs? Hurry and tell them they've stolen the son of a nobleman."

Arnold was tempted not to say anything. *If it had not been for Chad, I wouldn't be here being punished*, he thought. Then he thought of Timothy. What would Timothy do in Arnold's place?

He rushed out. "Chad," he called.

With a cry of recognition, Chad ran with wide-open arms to Arnold and hugged him. Arnold squeezed him hard. How could he ever have been angry with this terrified little boy?

"Take me home," Chad sobbed. "I don't want to be a friar."

When the abbot understood who Chad was, his face turned purple. "Take him to the manor house," he ordered a monk, but Chad sobbed louder and clung to Arnold like a burr.

"Then you take him," the abbot told Arnold. "Quickly, quickly." He turned to the visitors. "All this is exceedingly embarrassing to me. Sir Malcolm just sold some of his land to our monastery. Now, about the puppies. You say you each want one? I am sure we can arrange a satisfactory price."

On the way to the manor house, Arnold asked Chad what had happened. The story came out in a jumble of words. Timothy had left for Oxford to find a room for the coming school term. Chad had pleaded to go with him. Even before Sir Malcolm and John Wycliffe had left for London, Chad had run away, trying to follow his beloved older brother. He had walked and walked until he was tired, then sat by the roadside until the friars from Ipswich had come along and picked him up.

At the manor house entrance, Arnold heard the weeping and wailing of women.

"Lady Edith," he called. "Chad's here."

Chad ran to his mother's arms, and the whole household gathered around to hear the story. Sir Malcolm and John Wycliffe had not yet started for London, under the circumstances of Chad's disappearance.

Wycliffe paced the room, talking to Sir Malcolm. "The open theft of men's children by the religious orders under color of holiness must be sharply punished and forbidden, for by this many children have been damned instead of saved."

"You mean my baby might have been damned?" Lady Edith asked in horror. "Then why does the church have friaries and monasteries?"

"Christ commanded His apostles and disciples to preach the gospel," Wycliffe explained, "and not to close themselves in cloisters to pray, even though the founders of the various orders claimed that their members could no more dwell outside in the world than fish might dwell out of water." He added, "I anticipate that some of the friars whom God shall be pleased to enlighten will return with all devotion to the original religion of Christ, lay aside their unfaithfulness, and freely return to primitive truth and then build up the church as Paul did."

The abbot with his visitors called soon after, explained the story, with many apologies, then suggested a sum of money be paid as a tribute to God's watchfulness over His children.

John Wycliffe's head snapped back, and his eyes flashed fire. "How can you make money do the work of goodness? How can you set future blessedness up for sale?"

The abbot tried to say something, but Wycliffe was not to be silenced on his favorite theme.

"Christians must labor in some way for the good of society. You friars wallow in luxury. You look sharp after gold and silver plate, but shun work like poison. You preach jokes to beg better. You adulterate God's Word. And what is a monk? One who feeds his dogs and not the poor, keeping a fat horse with gay saddle and bridle. Half-dead men," he thundered.

Brother Kenningham tried to explain that Jesus begged.

Wycliffe stopped him. "Not open begging. The Dominicans say Christ had high shoes as they have. The Franciscans say Christ was barefoot, for otherwise Magdalene would not have washed Christ's feet. But Peter was not a barefooted friar. When he was in prison an angel told him to put on his shoes. You and other heretical idiots know not the sense of Scripture. The treasure of the Lord is hidden from simple priests, friars, and monks."

The abbot sniffed in anger. Arnold did not want to be the victim of the abbot's displeasure and slipped out of the house. On the way back to the monastery, a sudden thought struck him. Why not see Mother and Father first? Who would know the difference?

He ran to the cottage, pushed open the door, and stood still in blank amazement at the empty room, cold and damp. Where was Mother? He called, then looked outside. Nothing stirred. Puzzled, he turned back and noticed for the first time that the hearth fire was out. No cottager ever allowed that to happen. A cold fear ran up his spine. He ran to the fields and found Jock.

"My father and mother," he gasped. "Where are they?"

With a look of sympathy, Jock leaned on his hoe. "Why, lad, I suppose you couldn't have known, but they've left."

"You mean they are free?" Sudden joy replaced Arnold's previous fear.

Jock shook his head. "Not free, but they have a chance. You see," he explained, "if a man can hide in a city for a year and a day without being reclaimed by his lord, he is free."

"Where did they go?"

"Who knows? Perhaps London."

Arnold started off, confused thoughts whirling in his mind. Why should he go back to the monastery? Why couldn't he run away, too? In fact, why not be on his way right now before the abbot returned?

With a quick look all around, certain that no one noticed him, Arnold turned his back on the monastery and headed for the city of Oxford.

Doctor Wicked-Believe

5

After an all-day walk, Arnold joined a group of travelers near the north gate of Oxford. Peddlers, friars, beggars, and students lined up for admission to the city.

A student pointed out Balliol College outside the city walls. "That's where John Wycliffe took his Master of Arts degree," he told a companion. "Balliol is the oldest of the colleges."

"How about Merton College?"

Other students heard the discussion and told the dates of their colleges. It was finally agreed that the order was Balliol, Merton, Exeter, Oriel, University, and Queen's.

Would Wycliffe come to Balliol after his trip to London? Arnold looked at the sixteen-foot-deep fosse between the college and the walls and hoped Wycliffe would be in a college inside the city. Ahead, several college students jeered and hooted at the gatekeeper.

"Let us in! We're Oxford University students!"

"Break the gate down!"

"Break the gatekeeper's head, instead!"

A roar of laughter greeted the last suggestion.

"Why are the students rioting?" an alarmed traveler asked a peddler.

The peddler shrugged. "Any reason or no reason is enough for Oxford students."

The gatekeeper questioned some of the travelers. "Town or gown?"

"Gown," a young man ahead of Arnold proclaimed in a haughty tone. "I'm a student at Queen's College."

"Pass. But no rioting this year by order of the city commission."

"I'm a student at Merton College," the next student said.

"Were you in the riots last year?"

"What riots?"

The gatekeeper's face reddened. "Don't make mock of me. If you are an Oxford student, you know what rioting went on."

"Oh, you mean about Doctor Wicked-believe?"

"Doctor Wicked-believe?" the gatekeeper echoed. "Oh, you mean John Wycliffe."

"No, no," another student shouted. "His name is Doctor Evangelicus."

"Your Doctor whatever-his-name is under the protection of the king," the gatekeeper warned. "You Oxford students better watch your rioting."

"How could I riot?" a student explained in mock meekness. "I'm too busy studying mathematics, theology, grammar, rhetoric, and logic for my bachelor's degree."

Another chimed in. "And I studied arithmetic, music, geometry, and astronomy toward my master's. I have no time for rioting."

Arnold waited for his turn to be admitted. Someone pushed past him. A beggar, loathsome in his rags, used a crutch as a wedge and thrust his way to the head of the line. Murmurs and mutters from the

51

others followed in his wake. A student shoved the beggar from behind, but surprisingly, the beggar did not topple over. Instead, he raised up and brandished his crutch. At once other students turned, formed ranks, almost as if rehearsed, and with redoubled jeers and hoots, passed the beggar back.

If these students were aroused against John Wycliffe, would they act the same way? Arnold asked himself. Once inside the city, he watched students and other travelers disperse in all directions. Some headed for the inn, the Cardinal's Hat, just inside. Everyone seemed to know where he was going, all except Arnold.

He stumbled over the streets of rough stones, gaping at the narrow shops around the marketplace, the fishmongers' stalls in the middle of the street, the ducks waddling about, and the stone walls between every four or six wooden houses with vats of water before each door. Overhanging entries to houses darkened the streets. Soon night would fall. *Where will I sleep?* Arnold asked himself.

A voice droned. "Do you have a hall yet?"

A friar smilingly offered him an apple. Arnold knew that it was a bribe. He would not let himself be taken in by a friar.

"Queen's," he blurted and hurried away. He caught up with two students, determined to ask advice.

"There are several choices," he heard one say. "First, I could live in one of the university halls, but I don't want to do that. Too expensive. Second, I could live at an inn, but I don't want to do that either. Too noisy. Third, I could live with someone in town, and that's what I propose to do."

Arnold slumped into the doorway of a tailor shop, knees
to chin, when a girl suddenly asked,
"What are you doing here?"

"Find some tradesman's family," the other advised.

Arnold moved on. Night was coming fast. Did he dare go to any of these shuttered doors, so close to the street, and rap, or call up to some apartment overhanging the street and *beg*?

Discouraged, he slumped into the doorway of a tailor shop, knees to chin, feeling more alone than he ever had in his life. A sudden sympathy for beggars awoke in him. Maybe it was right that people looked at them as special objects of God's pity.

Footsteps rustled close to him.

"What are you doing there?" a girl asked.

Couldn't he even rest for a moment? Arnold thought in quick resentment.

"Well, move. I have to go in the shop."

This time he looked up. In the dusk he saw a girl younger than he holding a bundle by the corners of her large apron.

"Are you going to stay there all night?"

"No, I'll move," Arnold said wearily.

"Are you a student?"

"Yes and no."

"That's no answer. You look young, but sometimes students come here before they're fifteen. My name is Lucy Morris," she added.

"Mine's Arnold Hutton. I'm thirteen, my mother says." He added the courtesy statement, since ages were not supposed to be mentioned.

"I'm twelve, but that doesn't matter. What matters is I'm standing here with all these dirty shirts, and the students and professors want clean things before the opening mass on St. Martin's day. Are you hungry?" she wound up.

54

Arnold admitted he could eat.

"If my mother is home, I'll ask if you can eat with us. Sometimes she helps the tailor until very late. I'll leave the shirts here and find out." Lucy hurried into the shop and came out almost at once followed by a quick-moving woman.

"Come with us. I feed you in God's name," the woman said.

Her openhearted acceptance of him filled Arnold with relief and joy. He had not begged, and yet he had been offered the nourishment he needed. *Was this the way Jesus "begged"?* he thought, following Lucy upstairs.

After a supper of cheese, dark bread, and a porridge of peas, Arnold heard someone call from outside, "Dame Margot!"

Lucy's mother jumped up. "That's the tailor. What does he want at this hour?"

An old man puffed his way upstairs into the little apartment. "Three more orders for those russet-colored robes I told you about. Look. Here's one I just finished." He held up a robe with big patch pockets. "It's so strange. These students have money, I know. Why would they order such a common, ordinary color as *russet*?" The tailor's quavering scorn filled the room. "I tried to show them stuffs from Italy and even Scotland, but they would have none of it. Russet robes, they said, with big pockets. Why, I wouldn't clothe a beggar in this color. Some of those students are sons of noblemen. What do you make of it?"

Dame Margot did not know, and Arnold was not sure enough of what they meant, even though he remembered the two russet-clad young men at Sir

Malcolm's court, to try to explain. The tailor left shaking his head and wondering what young people were coming to. The mystery excited Arnold. He volunteered to help deliver clean laundry to the college halls, and in a short time, with Lucy's help, he learned to find his way around Oxford.

After one delivery, he heard two students talking on the street.

"Have you seen the Water Cliff?" one asked.

"The what?"

"They told me to ask to see the Water Cliff."

The other student burst into laughter. "Oh, you mean Wycliffe, the famous doctor here at Oxford. Wycliffe means water cliff, you know," he explained. "You can spell him *clif* or *clef* or *clyffe*, or *clyff*, or *kelf* — twenty different ways, and it still means Wycliffe, the one and only Doctor Wicked-believe."

Were students all over Oxford talking like this about Wycliffe? Arnold wondered. A cold wind whistled down the street. It seemed to bear a growing ill will with it. Did Wycliffe know what people were saying? Somehow, it did not seem important to Arnold anymore about trying to go to school. He would rather help John Wycliffe by keeping his eyes and ears open for threats against the good rector.

On October 9, after the feast of St. Denis, a group of students ran down the streets shouting, "Ban the ceremonies at St. Mary's."

Arnold, Lucy, and Dame Margot came out to watch.

Students erected a wooden cross and piled stones to keep it in place. Others lit candles, marched solemnly around the cross. Then one by one, each student dashed his candle to the ground.

56

Dame Margot was horrified. "Oxford students are mischievous, but they have never shown this kind of disrespect for the university that I remember."

The term opened the next day with the mass of the Holy Ghost at St. Mary's. Arnold and Lucy watched the procession.

"Look at their boots," Lucy told Arnold. "I don't know just how it is, but the kind they wear shows what year they are in."

Some wore boots to their middle leg. Others wore sandals or slippers.

"The masters all have powdered hair and long beards like soldiers," Lucy pointed out.

Three days later there was another procession and a mass for the king, queen, their children, and the peace of the university. The term was then under way.

From time to time, delivering laundry to various college halls, Arnold heard rumors about John Wycliffe's preaching in London. Students argued for and against Wycliffe's ideas about the Scripture being taught to simple people. News came that he would preach in Oxford on November 23.

When he arrived in Oxford, students gathered in the street. Arnold and Lucy joined them.

"He's coming this way," someone shouted.

"Which one is he? The one with the stooped shoulders?"

"Yes, and the big nose and long beard."

"He looks like a patriarch," a student commented. "Look how commandingly he walks."

"But how frail he is. A gust of wind would blow him away."

Without quite knowing how it started, Arnold heard the comments turn to jeers and mockery. The students surrounded Wycliffe, shouting taunts.

Wycliffe leaned on his staff, his shoulders more stooped than Arnold had ever seen them. Wycliffe's deep-set eyes seemed to probe the faces around him. His prominent nose curved like a bird's beak, and his sensitive mouth twitched above the full gray beard.

"You're a glutton when you eat!" a student taunted.

"Why, yes, I confess with pain that I eat frequently greedily, and delicately."

"You're a hypocrite when you fast," another threw out.

Wycliffe agreed. "If I were to try like a hypocrite to make false pretense about eating, they who sit with me at table would bear witness against me," was his mild reply.

Other taunts came fast.

"John Wicked-believe."

"Nay, call him Judas Scarioth."

"He speaks his views too strongly."

"Yes, before his disciples, but when he speaks before authorities, he backs down."

The students had blocked the street. Townspeople leaned out of second-story windows, or stood in shop doorways.

"He hides hatred but calls it holiness."

Wycliffe stood in silence before the student accusers.

"He has a quick temper."

This last jibe brought out a reply from Wycliffe. "I strive and pray about this, but it is too strong."

58

Somehow, this answer quieted the students, and they let Wycliffe go.

"Wycliffe says English money should not go to the Pope," someone called out. "He says England is no longer a milch cow."

The very students who had before jeered now applauded, but Arnold sensed that they would turn again at the slightest provocation. It was not long in coming.

"Let John Wycliffe, the heretic, hang!"

"What about John Wycliffe, the doctor?"

"Let him hang, too."

Uproar followed. The students started toward Wycliffe's hall. Arnold and Lucy were swept along, too. At the gate the students called for the gatekeeper to come out.

"Unlock the gates. Let us in. We have the right by the Magna Charta." Students pounded on the gate with sticks.

The gatekeeper opened a little window and thrust his head out. "Have the French landed? Oh, I see. It's just the Oxford students."

"Let us in, or we'll break in."

"You might as well go," the gatekeeper said. "I'm not unlocking this gate for anyone."

"You'll rue those words, my good man. Bishop Courtenay of London will send men and open the gates himself."

The gatekeeper laughed. "What are you here for?"

"We want Doctor Wycliffe, Doctor Wicked-believe."

The gatekeeper sniffed. "You can stay there the rest of your lives for all of me. You won't get in, and I'll see that the doctor does not come out."

"Then we'll batter down the gates."

"Try it. They're made of the sturdiest oak this side of the Lake country."

The students backed off and muttered among themselves. Someone grabbed Arnold's arm. "Arnold!" a familiar voice said. "What are you doing here?"

Arnold turned and found himself face-to-face with Timothy, whose blond hair was now clipped short in a clerk's tonsure.

Before Arnold could say anything, a blend of cheers and groans broke out. The students broke into two groups. A fist crashed into someone's cheekbones. The student flailed both hands to defend himself and hit someone behind him. At once a fight began. Pummeling, battering, using their heads to hammer at their opponents' stomachs, the students fought blindly. The wealthier ones tried to draw their belt knives, but the fighting was too close.

A trumpet sounded. The students stopped.

"Suppertime!"

Everyone rushed off to his own particular dining hall.

"Is it all a joke?" Arnold asked, bewildered.

"No," Timothy assured him. Later, at Dame Margot's, he paid for supper out of his pocket money and told Arnold, Lucy, and her mother about the growing plot to expel John Wycliffe from Oxford.

"But who are his enemies?" Dame Margot asked.

"I've been trying to find out," Timothy said. "Bishop Courtenay of London, for one, and I'm sure all four orders of friars here in Oxford have turned against him, even though he has a few individual friends among them. Then there'll be the Pope, if he hasn't already heard about Wycliffe."

"And is it all because Sir John wants people to know Scripture?" Arnold asked.

"Well, there are a few more things. Sir John has a strong opinion on many abuses of the church. He wants to correct them, but no one wants to be corrected, so they all want him expelled from Oxford."

"We'll have to help him someway," Arnold said. Everyone agreed. "But the question is, how?"

The Inner Room 6

Just what were the objections to John Wycliffe? Arnold hoped Timothy could find out by listening to the students during the day. A week later Timothy came to Dame Margot's with more details.

"Sir John believes God's grace is free. So why should friars beg poor people's money and then live a life of luxury? Then he says the Pope has forsaken the Word of God for human tradition." Timothy was checking off the points on his fingers. Arnold, Dame Margot, and Lucy sitting across from him at the table watched for each item.

"Next," Timothy continued, "priests have banished Scripture so that lay people hardly know there is such a thing as God's Word. Sir John keeps talking about restoring the Bible. I'm not sure just what he means."

"Is everyone in England against him?" Lucy asked, wide-eyed.

Timothy laughed. "Oh, no. The king's own brother, John of Gaunt, is his friend, but there must be people here in Oxford who are sending reports of Sir John's lectures to church prelates. But how and who?"

"We'll have to watch for spies," Arnold said.

Timothy nodded. "The *who* is the puzzle. Students are too busy to act as Rome-runners."

"As what?" Lucy asked.

"Pope's messengers who travel around delivering his bulls."

"Bulls?" Lucy's voice rose in disbelief.

"Not the kind that chased me last summer," Timothy grinned and rubbed his leg. "A bull is a document with the Pope's seal on it. His orders are more powerful than the king's." With a final reminder to the others to be alert to any strange happenings, Timothy invited Arnold to his college room the next afternoon.

The following day, in his eagerness to see Timothy, Arnold tripped over the outstretched legs of a beggar near the tailor shop.

"Look where you're going," the beggar growled. He picked up his crutch and waved it menacingly.

"Excuse me," Arnold began, then stopped. Why should he apologize to a beggar? A memory haunted him. Where had a beggar waved a crutch in this same way? Then he remembered the day he had entered Oxford. He looked more closely at the man's matted beard and hair. It was the same one, Arnold was sure. He went on down the street and looked back out of curiosity. The beggar was talking to a student. Very strange, he thought. Why wouldn't the beggar be down in the heart of the marketplace instead of by the tailor's shop?

In Timothy's room on the top floor of the hall, Arnold put the incident out of his mind. He examined the unglazed window with wooden shutters, the pan of charcoal for heating the room, the trestle table, and the shelf for books. A bed stood in the corner and rushes carpeted the floor.

When Arnold tripped over the outstretched legs of a beggar,
he picked up his crutch and growled,
"Look where you're going."

Arnold felt a twinge of envy.

"I've been thinking," Timothy said. "I'm permitted to have one servant. The two of us together might be able to find out more than each of us alone. On the other hand, you are free to go over the city when you deliver laundry for Dame Margot."

The boys discussed the possibilities. Arnold was tempted. It would be exciting to be among students all the time, but his strongest desire now was to help John Wycliffe. Why should such a truly God-loving man be hounded out of the place where he devoted so much time to teaching?

"Perhaps later," Arnold told Timothy. "I may be able to find out something on my own, first."

On the way back to Dame Margot's, Arnold heard a commotion inside a house. The door flew open. Two students in academic gowns were pushed outside by the broom of an irate housewife, whose ample apron covered an even more ample body. Keys dangling from a ring at her waist moved up and down with her vigorous arm movements.

"Get out and stay out of my house. I won't have the likes of you in here if I never have another Oxford student in my house again. And I'll tell that chancellor of yours why. The idea of plotting a student riot in my house! I won't have it now or any time."

As an afterthought, the housewife tossed out a pile of books and a heap of clothes. A few passersby gathered to watch.

"These Oxford students are getting so high and mighty they think they're above the law," one said.

The landlady launched into a vehement explanation. "Nowadays students think they can tell their elders what to do. They want to expel that poor, dear John Wycliffe. It's true he is outspoken, so I've heard, but that is no reason for turning him out of Oxford. He can spout Latin out of his ears, and that's more than these grubbing students can do. If they can construe two sentences out of four, they're doing well."

"Do you know Latin?" Arnold asked in surprise.

"I? No, of course not. But a body can't live in Oxford without hearing all about it." She gazed at him. "Are you looking for a room?"

"No, thank you." Arnold went on. How many other houses in Oxford harbored plotters against Wycliffe?

A few days later Timothy invited Arnold to a meeting John Wycliffe was holding in his room. When Arnold arrived, he found the room crowded with students. Their subdued chatter excited Arnold. What was this meeting about?

When Sir John entered, the students quieted.

"We have heard that this is a special group," someone said. "Tell us more about it. What do you mean?"

"I have in mind the words of Jesus according to Mark: 'And he said unto them, Go ye into all the world, and preach the gospel to every creature. He that believeth and is baptized shall be saved.'"

"Do you want us to become friars?"

Soft laughter circled the room. John Wycliffe's views on friars were well known.

Wycliffe hid a smile, then continued in a serious tone. "All believing people should have immediate access to Holy Scripture."

This time there was a gasp from the assembled students. "But what about the priests?"

"Christian truth is made known more clearly and accurately by means of Scripture than priests can declare it," Wycliffe went on.

The room buzzed with excited conjectures. "What does he mean?" student after student whispered.

"Evangelical preaching alone can stop the growth of sin," Wycliffe thundered. "It is more precious than the administration of any sacrament. By preaching, Christ effected more than by all His miracles."

"Yes, yes, Sir John, but tell us what this has to do with us. We don't have our degrees yet," a student pleaded.

But Wycliffe still did not explain what he meant. "Holy Scripture is the faultless, most true, most perfect, and most holy law of God, which men must know, defend, and observe. No man can become righteous and well pleasing to God who does not hold to God's law. The sowing of God's Word is the appointed means for the glory of God and edification of our neighbor."

Arnold watched the baffled faces of the others. He was sure what John Wycliffe had in mind.

"There are three kinds of pastors," Wycliffe said. "Some are true both in name and truth, some only in name. Of these, some preach for fame; some fail duties but do no harm, and some rob the poor and incite them to sin. The real shepherd shows the way, heals the sick, feeds the hungry by preaching and opening the wisdom of Scripture."

Preaching. A number of students had caught on to the key idea.

"How can this be done?"

"The true preacher must address himself to the heart, so as to flash the light into the spirit of the hearer and to bend his will into obedience to the truth."

"Do — do you want *us* to *preach*?" The question seemed to hang in space.

"Why, yes. Proclaim the gospel without desire of gain. Preach openly to the people that God counts more by works of mercy in a man's soul than by offerings or tithes or other goods given to friars."

"Your preachers then will be beggars?" was the next question. A kind of tingling filled the room. Arnold felt the suppressed excitement of the students when one by one they understood what John Wycliffe was proposing.

"These preachers will not openly beg, as do the mendicant friars, but will live on what is offered them," Wycliffe explained.

"What are their duties? How are they to be trained? Will you train them?" The questions bubbled up from all sides. "What will they be called?"

"Poor Priests," Wycliffe said. "The first general rule of the Poor Priests is that the law of God be well known, taught, maintained, and magnified. The second is that the great open sin that reigns in England be destroyed. The third is that the true peace, prosperity, and burning charity be increased in Christendom. Christian men must study, keep, teach, and maintain Holy Writ more than they do new statutes, customs, and sermons made of sinful men."

In the discussion that followed, some students

slipped out of the room. Others clamored to hear more about the Poor Priests and their garb of russet. Some pledged themselves to go as soon as Wycliffe trained them.

Arnold knew that he and Timothy were too young to even think about being a Poor Priest, but he knew, too, with a sudden, utter conviction, that in a few years he would be one of the eager disciples of Christ.

A student asked Wycliffe point-blank, "What about your enemies among the prelates? Will they permit you to carry out these heretical ideas?"

Wycliffe laughed. "They haven't stopped me yet." He seemed totally unconcerned about the possibility of enemies striking back at him.

Arnold remembered Wycliffe's indifference a few days later. At the river Lucy had dumped the big wooden bucket of dirty shirts on the ground. With the deftness of much experience, she shook out some coins, a knife, and several quill pens from the pile of shirts. Arnold ran his hand over the finely woven linen of one shirt. What would it feel like to wear such expensive clothes? One sleeve, thicker than the other, rustled in his fingers. Something had been rolled up and sewn in an inner pocket.

"There's something in this shirt, Lucy."

She ran her fingers over it. "I've never felt anything like this before."

"It's paper, or parchment," Arnold tugged at the big stitches. "There's writing on it." He pulled out the paper and examined it.

"What does the writing say?"

Arnold read the letter and jumped to his feet. "Sir

John won't be indifferent now. It's a copy of a letter from a man named Adam Easton to Abbot Litlington of Westminster. He wants the abbot to have his monk-students at Oxford send him — it says here — 'a copy of the sayings of a certain master John Wycliffe, which he disseminates, as it is said, against our order in Oxford.' Then he wants copies of two more of Wycliffe's works." Arnold read the letter again. "Sir John must have this letter. This will prove to him that people are trying to expel him from Oxford."

"Hide the letter someplace," Lucy said. "We have to get the washing done first."

Arnold fastened the letter inside his own shirt and helped Lucy beat the dirty clothes with wooden paddles.

A boat being punted up the river stopped by Arnold and Lucy. One college student was punting and the other stood poised on the gunwale, bent over, ready to jump on land. The boat nosed to the shore, and the student leaped from the boat, scrambled up the bank, and began pawing over the shirts.

"Stop that," Lucy shouted. "What are you doing?"

"I can't find it," the student panted to the boatman.

"Look again," the second student said. "I told you not to put it there. If it's found, we'll both be expelled. You were foolish to make a copy in the first place. Anything in writing is dangerous. All I can say is find it, find it."

The first student glared at Arnold and Lucy. "Did you find a letter in these shirts?"

The secret letter seemed to burn Arnold's skin. He

70

could not lie, and he could not say yes. Instead he turned his back.

"They don't know anything," the boatman said in disgust. "It must be in your room."

Lucy watched the students leave. "I've never had anything like this happen in all my life. That letter must be very important."

"Where can we hide it for the time being?" Arnold asked. "Isn't there an inner room behind the tailor's shop?"

"Yes, but don't go in there," Lucy warned.

"It would be a good hiding place, so why not?"

"Because I know a secret about it."

"Lucy, this letter is enough secret for me," Arnold said in disgust.

"Aren't you going to ask me what the secret is?"

"Then it wouldn't be a secret, would it?"

"No, I suppose not, but just don't go in there. The tailor is letting a man and a woman stay in that room."

"Oh." Arnold was astonished. He had not noticed anyone go in or out.

"And I think they're *lepers*," Lucy whispered.

Arnold winced at the dreaded word. "What makes you think so?"

"Because they never come out in the daytime, only at night, although sometimes the woman goes to market. Maybe she isn't a leper, but he must be, because my mother told me I must never go in there."

Then Arnold began putting two and two together. The tailor was filling orders for russet gowns. What if the news about the Poor Priests had reached the ears of Wycliffe's enemies?

71

He told Timothy about the inner room later. Timothy was doubtful about the couple being spies. They did sound strange, he admitted. But the letter was something else. Timothy promptly took it and hid it in his own clothes. "I'll put it somewhere safe," he promised. "I think Sir John has gone to London again. When he comes back I'll give it to him."

The next evening Lucy told Arnold more about the couple in the inner room. "It's a runaway man."

Arnold's ears tingled. "Runaway from where?"

"I don't know, but the tailor gave him some robes to sew and he's sewing. His wife sews, too."

"How long have they been here?" Arnold's voice quavered with his sudden hope.

"Just a few days. They're very nice."

Still later she added another bit of information. "He's a runaway bondman, and if his lord doesn't find him after a year and a day, he's free."

Arnold did not tell Lucy what he was hoping for. If she couldn't keep a secret, he could. When she left, he went in to talk to the tailor. A customer came into the shop, and Arnold tiptoed to the back room and listened. He could hear low voices inside. He tapped on the door. The voices stopped.

"It's Arnold," he called, and waited. Who would open the door? Would it be Father and Mother?

The door opened. Arnold found himself face-to-face with Sir Malcolm. Timothy stood behind his father, and there at one side, facing him, stood Father and Mother.

A sickening realization came over Arnold. The year and a day was far from being up. Sir Malcolm had found Father and Mother. They would not be free after all. Arnold would have to go back to the monastery. And what about Timothy? Had he found out who the "spies" were — and told?

The Gospel Doctor 7

Arnold tried to hide his dismay, but accusing thoughts raced through his mind. Why had he ever thought high and low rank could ever mix — even for a worthy, common cause like helping John Wycliffe? Timothy was certainly within the law to tell his father about a runaway bondman. But Timothy did not even show concern. In fact, he seemed quite happy.

"Don't look at me like that, Arnold," Timothy said in his usual calm way. "I had no idea your father and mother were here until one of the Poor Priests sent me to pick up his new russet robe and your father brought it out. Besides, my father has something to explain."

Little by little the story took shape. Sir Malcolm had come to Oxford to find out what Timothy had heard about John Wycliffe's enemies. He had found out that Timothy was at the tailor's, had come there, and found the Huttons.

"But your father is now a free man," he hastened to explain. The reeve had confessed to taking rent and tax money and exchanging white tally sticks for it, and even now was in the stocks with hands and feet dangling.

Father and Mother had gone first to London, had heard Wycliffe preach there about the gospel, and had come to Oxford to be near him and help if they could.

By this time, the tailor himself stood listening at the door. Dame Margot and Lucy peeked in, and when the tailor invited Father to stay on permanently to help with the orders — "more orders than I can handle. You're a godsend, and you can have all the russet robes to tailor" — Arnold felt a strength and inner peace he had never known before. God was really on their side!

Arnold remembered something. "What about the letter?"

"Timothy gave it to me," Sir Malcolm said. "I'm taking it right now to Sir John, and then I'm leaving for London. I was to have met Sir John there this week, but he was apparently detained here. Sometimes I wish he would just stay in his room and write, but between his teaching and his preaching, he's really stirring everyone up. If he would just realize that he has enemies!"

Later, Timothy came to Dame Margot's with startling news. "Someone stole the letter from my father — right there at the hall. He didn't even get to show it to Sir John, and now Father has gone to London. He's really worried, and thinks it would be a good idea, Arnold, if you would stay with me as if you were a servant. We've got to find out who is sending reports of his lectures to prelates all over England."

Timothy was more upset than Arnold had ever seen him.

"Father said Sir John's name was on everyone's lips, and he heard the students talk about some of the astonishing things Sir John says," Timothy continued.

"Like what?" Lucy asked.

"Well, like saying that the bread and wine in the

mass are not the body of Christ. Sir John says the very mice know that bread is bread."

"Isn't that what's called *heresy?*" Dame Margot asked.

"Decidedly," Timothy said. "Sir John can't help but make enemies with such views."

Timothy's mention of enemies reminded Arnold of the letter. "What are we going to do about it?"

"Well, there isn't any letter to show Sir John, so there is nothing we can do."

But Arnold was not convinced. That night he tried to remember what the letter said. If Timothy could remember parts of it, too, they could at least put Sir John on his guard.

The next morning, starting out for Timothy's, Arnold saw two of Wycliffe's russet-clad Poor Priests talking to passersby. He called to Lucy to come out.

"What!" she said in scorn after one look. "Have you brought me out here just to hear some *beggars?*"

"They're not beggars, exactly. They're preachers. They preach from the Bible."

"The beggars' Bible," Lucy jeered.

"Lucy, they don't beg openly. They are rich students who are giving up all they have to preach the truth about God. They carry Scripture in their pockets and read from it the most marvelous stories."

"No beggar is going to tell me anything," Lucy announced with a toss of her head, "but I love to hear stories." She called her mother to come out, too.

One of the Poor Priests looked right at Lucy. "Once there was a boy about your age who was so intelligent that He astonished learned doctors of His time. He told them things they didn't even know."

"They didn't know?" Lucy echoed. "Grown men, you mean? What happened then?"

"These grown men admitted in front of everyone that this boy knew more than they. And, Miss, this boy became a king."

"Did He, now? King?" Lucy's eyes sparkled.

"Yes, a king, but not of this world."

"How could that be?" Dame Margot asked.

"It was so, and is so. It is written here." The Poor Priest pulled out a scroll and read the story from Scripture.

"That's beautiful. Why doesn't our priest read to us like this?" Lucy asked. "Are there more stories?"

"Many, many more, telling of God's love for man and how He wants everyone to know and follow His law."

When the two young men left, Lucy looked after them wistfully. "I hope the beggar-priests come back," she said. "I would like to hear the other stories from the beggars' Bible."

Arnold went on to Timothy's hall, but Timothy was out. Arnold went on to Wycliffe's room in Black-hall and found John Purvey, an assistant to Wycliffe.

"Sir John has an enemy," Arnold told him.

Purvey, serious-faced and intent, nodded. "That is not strange. Who?"

"It was in a letter."

"May I see it?"

"The letter was stolen." Arnold was beginning to be embarrassed. How weak his explanation must sound to Purvey! "It was from Adam Easton."

"Ah!" The exclamation from Purvey told Arnold the letter was important. "The Hebraist cardinal at

Avignon. Go on. What did the letter say?"

"He wrote to Abbot Litlington of Westminster, and he called him a 'black dog.' "

"That's strange."

"I mean Sir John called the abbot a black dog," Arnold hurried to explain. "He said his whelps were responsible for proceedings at the Curia." Arnold hoped Purvey would understand.

Purvey sat on a bench and clasped his hands around one knee. "Go on."

"The letter wants the abbot to get his monk-students at Oxford to send him a copy of Sir John's sayings."

Purvey laughed. "Which ones? Sir John preaches, teaches, and writes."

"The ones against the abbot's order here in Oxford," Arnold explained, happy that he could remember so much of the letter.

"Ah!"

"And he wants copies of two more of Sir John's works on civil and divine lordship."

Purvey stood up and rubbed his hands. "This is of great help. Now, how can we get the letter?"

Arnold sighed. That would be next to impossible. Would Sir John believe there was such a letter and realize his enemies were going to use it against him?

A few days later Sir John himself came to the tailor shop and ordered a russet robe. A rumble outside jarred the room. The tailor hurried to the door. "What is happening? I have never in my life seen such unrest here in Oxford. What is it all leading to?" Then he grunted. "I see what it is now, just Oxford students rolling a barrel with stones in it."

"Good sirs, I have here a pardon hot from Rome. What
will you offer?"

Wycliffe's assistant, John Purvey, hurried in. "Sir John, I've come to take you back to your hall. You must come right away."

"What is it now?" Wycliffe sighed. "Have you uncovered more problems?"

"The students are gathering on the street. It looks like an uprising."

"Just a college prank," Wycliffe said. Nevertheless, he waited until the street was quiet and went out with Purvey. Arnold followed.

Faster than a shadow, a brown-robed begging friar stepped from a doorway. "Alms for the poor, in God's name," he intoned, holding out a stick with a little bag attached.

Purvey dropped in a coin.

"Thanks be to God for His mercy." The friar raised his eyes to the sky.

The friar, with a sly look, then pulled out a rolled paper. "Good sirs, I have here a pardon hot from Rome. What will you offer?"

"Iscariot!" Wycliffe snapped and tried to pass. "You friars sell Christ as Judas did."

The friar tugged at Wycliffe's long sleeve. "Let not your sins lead you to purgatory."

Wycliffe jerked away, then, with eyes flashing, he turned to the friar. "Am I to pay you and your kind for stolen bulls, false relics, and lap dogs for the ladies? What about your rule, which forbids you to touch coin?"

The friar stood paralyzed at Wycliffe's thundering words.

"This is John Wycliffe," Purvey said with a hint of a smile.

The friar backed away as if he had touched poison.

"You profess poverty," Wycliffe continued. "Look at your portable altar, your absolutions, your sale of pardons, your special prayers for the souls of the dead, all for money. Is this the poverty spoken of by Christ?"

The friar turned, but Wycliffe stepped in front of him. "You shrive men of sins they are ashamed of confessing to their own pastor."

John Wycliffe walked on with the friar, preaching all the way. Arnold started to catch up with Purvey, but a beggar clutched Arnold's hand and pulled him downward.

"Alms," he hissed, his bearded face almost next to Arnold's. "Alms, for the love of God."

It was the same beggar. For a wild moment, Arnold was sure Oxford had no other beggars than this one man.

Arnold struggled to free himself, but the beggar's surprisingly sturdy arm held him like a vise. In a half stoop, Arnold realized the beggar was not interested in alms. He was using Arnold as a shield to hide himself from John Wycliffe, who had looked around for Purvey.

The beggar clutched Arnold even tighter, his bright eyes rolling in his bearded face like candles shining on a church altar. Then the beggar pushed Arnold away and lapsed into his former slump, head down, fingers dangling from his knees, his crutch at his side.

Something about the beggar puzzled Arnold, he told Timothy later. Arnold had looked back and seen a student talking to the beggar. "And that has happened before, too. Why would a student stop to talk to a beggar?"

"To give him alms, of course."

Arnold sighed: Of course. Most people believed God sent beggars to test their charity and insure their going to heaven.

"Still, it sounds like the same beggar who came to the hall last night. An odd thing happened," Timothy admitted. "This fellow on his crutch — " Timothy limped to show how the beggar walked — "wanted something to eat. So the steward gave him to eat out of the poor man's plate, and the beggar wouldn't take it."

The beggar and his crutch again. Why did that beggar haunt the college area instead of the marketplace?

Who was the beggar? Once again Timothy, Arnold, and Lucy sat at the table upstairs in Dame Margot's apartment and talked. Dame Margot herself was at the marketplace to shop.

"Who could he be?" Arnold mused.

"Go ask him," Lucy said impetuously.

The boys looked at her in scorn.

"Well, sometimes you ask a person right out and he answers," she defended herself.

"I suppose spies go right up to Sir John and ask him if he is a heretic," Arnold retorted.

Timothy was calm. "We'll have to figure it out first and then confront him."

"All right. First we know that he acts very strange, even for a beggar," Lucy said.

All agreed.

"Next, we know that he talks to students a lot."

A sudden understanding came to Arnold. "That's it!

He *sounds* like a student! He talks like a student! That's what was puzzling me. He's an educated beggar!"

The three stared at each other. Timothy admitted the beggar did not sound like the ordinary kind.

"Would Bishop Courtenay have sent him to spy on Wycliffe?" Arnold mused.

"Why would he send a beggar instead of a real student who could mingle with the others?" Timothy asked.

"Because a beggar moving over the country would be better able to find out how many Poor Priests Sir John is sending out," Arnold said.

Dame Margot hurried in from marketing. "The students are gathering in the marketplace. There's going to be an uprising against Sir John."

Arnold ran downstairs to warn his parents and the tailor. Timothy, Lucy, and Dame Margot followed. Everyone watched from the doorway.

From a distance, a soft, uneasy murmur grew more and more agitated. A group of Oxford students poured around a corner. They marched shoulder to shoulder, blocking the entire street.

The tailor grunted. "So we have to go through this again. Fall, winter, or spring, something gets in their blood. They break out of their dingy dark rooms, and then in a few hours it's all over."

The noise from the students grew louder, more threatening. The tailor listened.

"They sound different this time. I know there has been talk about John Wycliffe, but I don't see how college students can do anything more than noisy mischief."

A loud crash silenced him.

The tailor frowned. "How many of those students are studying to be priests?"

"Most of them," Timothy said.

Arnold stepped outside to see how close the students were.

"Come back. We'll have to close and shutter the door," the tailor called.

But Arnold had seen the beggar seated in a doorway, crutch by his side. Torn with disgust and shame for his feeling of loathing toward a cripple, embarrassed at having accused him of being some kind of spy against John Wycliffe, Arnold took a step forward to warn the beggar.

At that moment the cripple let out a yell, jumped up, leaving his crutch, and ran to greet the leader of the revolt.

"Silence the teacher of heresy!" he yelled, and the mob took up the cry. "Down with the gospel doctor."

Double Trouble 8

The fierce rhythm of the student marchers bounced through the soles of Arnold's feet. How easy it would be to join such a group without thinking, just for the tingling excitement of action!

"We've got to warn Sir John," Timothy shouted. "Come on!" He darted out of the shop with Arnold close behind.

At Blackhall, Timothy panted a warning to the porter. "We must tell Sir John."

The porter was unmoved. "I'm afraid you won't be able to see him. The good doctor is preparing to receive a very distinguished visitor. A messenger came from London not an hour ago."

"But the students are rioting."

"They've done that before."

"But they're after Sir John," Arnold said in desperation.

"Here is Sir John, now, I think, but it is a pity he has been disturbed."

John Wycliffe stood at the bottom of the stairs, his eyebrows raised in questioning. "What is it?" he asked in such quiet tones that Arnold doubted his own senses. Wycliffe usually was far more excited on hardly any pretext, yet here in the face of danger he was calm. Or hadn't he realized there was danger?

"The students are rioting, Sir John," the porter said matter-of-factly. "According to these boys, they're on their way here."

"When they arrive, tell them it is against the rules to riot."

"But Sir John, they won't be turned off with words," Timothy pleaded. "They want *you*."

"What are they saying?"

Arnold repeated the words of the beggar who wasn't a beggar, and described him to Wycliffe.

" 'Silence the teacher of heresy,' " Wycliffe mused. "I remember that so-called beggar. He was expelled from Oxford once. I wonder who authorized his return as a student? In any case, he can't do much harm." Wycliffe invited the boys to dine at the hall that night. "I'm expecting a friend of your father's," he told Timothy, and then went upstairs.

The first sounds of the student riot drifted through the doorway of Blackhall like the faraway rustle of leaves in a high wind, together with an occasional piercing shriek or high-pitched laughter. Servants gathered to listen. The steward, however, was more concerned about the dinner that night for the distinguished guests.

"Take great care," he warned his kitchen help. "Don't forget the cloth under the wine flagon. Remember to let him uncover the bread. Are the salt-cellars filled? The trenchers clean?" A spasm shook him. "Why wasn't I warned ahead of time? If anything goes amiss, we'll all be put in the stocks." He went off muttering and checking items off on his fingers.

Arnold heard a new sound from outside. Half-groan, half-taunt, the noise grew more intense, accompanied by the steady shuffle of people carrying something heavy. The servants bolted the doors and stared at each other, the same question written on every face. If the students broke through the huge double doors, where could members of the hall flee? They ran to find weapons for defense.

A fierce blow shook the door, then another, and another. The students must have found a tree trunk, taken off the limbs, and used it to batter the door. The next minute the doors were flung open. The leaders, stunned momentarily by the sudden release of the heavy wooden barrier, stood blinking at the servants lined up with wooden bats, heavy pans, and even wooden trenchers to defend themselves and the honor of the college hall.

The hubbub stopped for a moment. The students sounded surprised.

"What say you to this?" a rioter called in insolent tones.

"Good sirs, I pray you — " the porter began.

"O! fie! for shame!" a student sneered.

"Gentlemen! On behalf of — "

Trumpets sounded outside, but they were not the dinner call. The rioters looked, gasped, and divided ranks. Four outriders in royal livery, banners fluttering from their trumpets, rode up to the door. Then a tall man, elegantly dressed, followed by at least twenty armed men, dismounted. The students pressed back to make room.

"It's John of Gaunt," the awed whisper ran. "The king's own brother."

"It can't be true."

"But it is. Look at those liveries. No one can mistake the royal colors."

"Why has he come to Oxford?"

"To see Wycliffe, of course. They've been friends for years."

With mumbles and bows, the students drifted away. Where had the rebellion gone?

When the doors to the dining hall opened, the student residents did not pour in pell-mell as they usually did. Instead, they pressed near the walls. A subdued murmur spread over the group. In impressive silence, John of Gaunt, tall and imposing, his long mantle sweeping in a semicircle about him, strode to the entrance of the room, glanced around, and with an imperious wave, summoned John Wycliffe and went directly to the high table. The college students took their own places at the long tables beneath. Arnold and Timothy sat at the far end and grinned at each other. With John of Gaunt in Oxford, no riot would take place.

A few days later the reason for John of Gaunt's visit was made plain.

"They're going to try Sir John for heresy," Timothy told Arnold.

"Where? When?"

"In London, at St. Paul's."

After February 19, 1377, news of the trial filtered back to Oxford. The tailor, Arnold's parents, Dame Margot, and Lucy picked up bits of information here and there.

"They say Bishop Courtenay wouldn't let him sit down." Lucy said one evening when all were at supper in Dame Margot's apartment.

"I heard that John of Gaunt had representatives from the four orders of friars," Timothy began.

"Oh, how terrible!" Lucy said. "Sir John doesn't like friars."

"He doesn't like what they do," Timothy corrected, "but he has many friends among them. These friars were there to defend him."

"Oh," Lucy said. "Then Sir John can come back to Oxford?"

"Yes. He's already here."

Dame Margot contributed a bit of news. "I heard that John of Gaunt was going to drag Bishop Courtenay out of St. Paul's by the hair."

"And there was a huge crowd there, and they were all for Sir John, and they want more of his gospel teaching," Dame Margot said.

"Was Sir John freed?" the tailor asked. "Will he be able to go on with his Poor Priests?"

"Yes," the others chorused. All agreed that nothing really harmful had happened to Sir John's training of Poor Priests. With such powerful friends as John of Gaunt, who would be able to object to John Wycliffe's preaching, teaching, and writing?

"But someone *is* objecting," Timothy told Arnold months later. Again the Oxford students were meeting on the streets. Again copies of a letter were being passed around. Arnold remembered the other letter he and Timothy could never find after it was taken.

"Sir John won't care," Arnold said.

"But this one is from the Pope."

Arnold gasped in quick concern. The Pope's word was greater than the king's.

"What does it say?"

One angry student leader in the mob waved a paper over his head, "This will put Wycliffe out of Oxford forever."

"Some students are meeting outside Sir John's hall today. I think they're going to read it."

"I'll be there, then," Arnold promised.

At the meeting, a student leader waved a paper over his head. "This will put Wycliffe out of Oxford forever."

A cheer broke out among the assembled students. "Read it; read it."

"It's too long to read except in part, but the Pope says Wycliffe has rashly burst forth in detestable madness — "

A groan, partly of assent, partly of dissent interrupted the speaker.

"His conclusions are erroneous and false — "

"Aye, aye," the students called out.

"He is malignantly infecting Christ's faithful and causing them to deviate from Catholic faith, without which there is no salvation."

A strong voice broke in. "Let Sir John defend himself publicly in a lecture hall."

Surprisingly, the students agreed. Arnold had learned from Timothy of the Oxford custom of having students reason before the public, even if the latter had to be dragged in from the street to act as audience.

Wycliffe agreed to defend his views, and Timothy was able to arrange for Arnold to be present in one of the lecture halls. While they waited, two graduate students behind Arnold and Timothy began to talk.

"I hear the friars have turned against Wycliffe," one said. "Just last February at the trial all four orders defended him, and I know he has always been on particularly good terms with the Franciscans."

The other agreed. "But I believe it was the Dominicans who first detected his heresy — William Jordan and Roger Dimock, to say nothing of Robert Humbleton who has out and out declared he was an enemy to Wycliffe."

"How about the Carmelites?"

"Oh, Kenningham took up the cry. He said Wycliffe was being guided by the house of Herod."

The lecture hall was gradually filling up with students and even townspeople had obtained permission to sit in on the discussion.

The students behind Arnold and Timothy started to talk about the Poor Priests.

"What do you know about this 'Poor Priests' evangelical crusade?" one asked.

"Better call it the beggars' evangelical crusade," the other suggested with a snort of disgust. "It may have started as early as 1368, when Wycliffe was at Ludgarshall."

"But that was nine years ago," the other student exclaimed. "Do you mean those russet-clad beggars have been invading the countryside all this time?"

"Who can say when first the devil enters a man?"

Another student joined in. "I don't think Wycliffe's Poor Priests started out before this spring."

"I still say beggars," the first said. "What do they really do?"

"They carry around tracts and skeletons of sermons written by Wycliffe, and paraphrases of the Bible."

While he waited with the others for John Wycliffe to appear, Arnold was remembering what Wycliffe had said months before about God's will. Was it God's will that Wycliffe be tried for heresy and called on to defend himself for doing the very thing God wanted — the spreading of His Word? Why didn't God make it easier for Sir John? If everyone were going to continue accusing him, how could Wycliffe know he was following God's law?

The question haunted Arnold. What was his own future part in the work to be?

A student leader came in with Wycliffe and immediately opened the meeting.

"We know that Pope Gregory XI has signed five bulls against John Wycliffe of Oxford and Lutterworth. We know that there are nineteen charges against John Wycliffe. In his bull addressed to the University of Oxford, the Pope laments the fact that the authorities here have permitted tares to spring up amongst the wheat of Oxford's famous soil, and not only that, but more pernicious, the tares have been allowed to mature without being rooted out. Still, to be fair, we should hear the doctor himself."

Wycliffe smiled slightly. "This is like breaking a man's head and then handing him a healing plaster."

A ripple of amusement spread over the room.

"From the eleventh century on, the dogma of the church has been perverted," Wycliffe declared. "Rome has built up a superstructure on the true foundation. We must sweep it away and get back to the life and words of Christ. Should not Christ be known to every man?"

"Take the doctor away," a student in the audience shouted.

Wycliffe smiled again. "He leaves the question unanswered, like the woman who, when asked how far is it to Lincoln answered, 'A bag full of plums.'"

The laughter from the crowd was more open.

"Don't argue with him," another student shouted. "To argue with Wycliffe, a *profundus clericus*, is like little boys throwing stones at the Pleiades."

This remark did not stop other students in the attentive audience.

"You are defying the Pope," one said. "But you must admit there must be a head of the church here on earth."

"If you say that Christ's church must have a head here on earth, true it is, for Christ is the head. He is here with His church unto the day of doom. And if you say that Christ must have a vicar such as the Pope here on earth, then you deny Christ's power and make such a fiend above Christ."

There was a gasp at Wycliffe's strong term.

"But your doctrine leads everyone astray," still another student said.

"My doctrine? Let us follow the example of Lord Jesus Christ, who was humble enough to confess, 'My doctrine is not Mine, but the Father's who sent Me.'" He continued, "God is much more than any lord of earth. He sent a letter to man by Moses, His messenger, that is worth more than any message by Pope or cardinal and better than a letter with the king's seal, for His service is light and His heritage is much, for it is the bliss of heaven everlasting, without end."

The audience rustled in agreement.

"We must stir men from sin and draw them to virtue through knowledge of Holy Scripture. The day of doom shall come to us, and we know not how soon. How busy we should be to make ready! We must fasten in us articles of the truth, for they are as loose in us as nails in a tree. It is needful to knock and make them fast."

Wycliffe was talking at his full power now. His slight body rocked with his deep feeling.

"We must cry aloud, spare not, show people their sins. The sin of common people is great, but the sin of the mighty and wise is greater, and most blinding of all is the sin of prelates."

The audience sat silent until someone asked how sin could be overcome.

"No man can become righteous and well-pleasing to God who does not hold to God's law."

Wycliffe had hardly finished these words when there was a flurry of movement at the entrance. The Vice-Chancellor of Oxford, a monk, ordered the meeting closed.

As everyone filed out, Arnold heard the Vice-Chancellor tell Wycliffe to come with him at once to Blackhall. The monk must have underestimated the audience who had been listening to Wycliffe. They were waiting outside on the street. A rumor sped quickly among the onlookers.

"In chains, the Pope said."

"He didn't want anybody to know about the arrest, though."

People stopped the student leader and asked if it were true that Wycliffe was to be arrested.

"Yes, until there are further instructions from the Pope."

Arnold and Timothy watched Wycliffe quietly submit to arrest. In anger and despair, Arnold could only ask one question. "Why?"

Sowing the Word 9

With John Wycliffe imprisoned, what would happen to the Poor Priests?

Arnold sat with his mother, Dame Margot, and Lucy in the upstairs apartment next to the tailor shop and discussed the action brought about by the Pope.

"But the Poor Priests have already spread the hope of the gospel over England. Can anything really stop that?" Dame Margot asked. "Right here in Oxford everyone I know wants to learn more about Scripture. John Wycliffe's good work can't stop."

"It won't stop," Arnold's mother said with conviction.

The tailor and Arnold's father came upstairs late.

"Some students were in asking questions and fingering every bolt of cloth in the shop. Then they went away without ordering anything," Father said, puzzled.

"Not even a russet robe," the tailor sighed.

"They weren't Poor Priests coming after their robes, then?" Dame Margot asked.

"No, and not only that, but we have six russet robes ready and no one has claimed them."

"They're afraid of persecution," Dame Margot said.

Timothy rushed upstairs. "There's smoke coming out of the tailor shop!"

Everyone rushed down. A fire smoldered in a pile

of scraps. The two boys and the two men chain-passed wooden buckets of water from the nearest vat of water standing ever ready for dreaded fires. The fire was soon put out.

Dame Margot shook her head. "A dab of water like that wouldn't help much if a fire had really started," she said. "There isn't enough water in the Cherwell or Thames either to put out the fire in some people's hearts," she added.

In the excitement, Timothy had almost forgotten the news he was bringing. "Sir John's imprisonment isn't a real one."

"You mean he's free?" Lucy asked.

"No, he isn't free."

"Then he's imprisoned."

"It's really voluntary," Timothy explained. "You see, the Pope ordered him to be 'seized and incarcerated,' as *he* said, but England can't give the Pope that much power, because then the Pope would act like a king. The authorities had to do something about the Pope's orders, though, so the Vice-Chancellor just asked Sir John if he would stay in Blackhall and not go out, so that no one else could arrest him."

Lucy clenched her fists and pounded on the table in excitement. "Why didn't he fight back? Why didn't he say no?"

"He said he could write just as well in Blackhall as he ever could, and he didn't mind not going out. He didn't seem a bit disturbed by it all."

Another time Timothy brought more news to the group. "Sir John had to go to London and answer some questions. The queen mother ordered Bishop Courtenay not to take any decided measures against

Sir John. Then a lot of people broke into the chapel where the meeting was and carried Sir John away."

"Isn't it strange how God seems to be protecting him?" Mother said.

Arnold decided there was an answer to his "why?" at the first news of Sir John's imprisonment. Sir John was settled once more in Oxford and going ahead with his training of Poor Priests. At a meeting in Sir John's room, Arnold met several associates of Sir John's. There was John Purvey and Nicholas Hereford, whom he knew. Others were Philip Repingdon, whose friends called him the most learned among them. Other names Arnold learned were John Thoresby, Uhtred Bolton, Walter Bryt, and Philip Norris.

At this meeting, Sir John was downstairs for a long time talking with the Chancellor. Upstairs in his room, Sir John's associates talked among themselves.

"Is Sir John going to Rome?" John Thoresby asked Hereford.

"No. Why should he?"

"The Pope gave him three months in which to appear there, I understand."

"What can the Pope really do if the king's authorities don't want to take action?"

A heated discussion began. When Sir John came in, one of the young men asked Sir John what he thought of the Pope's statement that he was killing souls.

"I am ignorant of any open crime laid to my charge," Sir John said. "I shall patiently endure reproach. Just as God passes man, so God's law must pass in authority anything man sets up." He thought a moment. "A cord is a good thing, and a fast knot is good for both man and beast in places where it will do good, but knot this cord about a man's throat and it can soon strangle him."

Someone mentioned how previous friends of Sir John's had dropped away, afraid of persecution.

Wycliffe admitted the fact. "Some men fail in faith, for it is so thin. Christ oftentimes reproved His apostles for the littleness of their faith when they failed to trust in Him."

Still, there were new faces in the group, Arnold could see. Sir John talked enthusiastically about returning to Christ's teachings.

"How did people turn away?" Philip Repingdon, the most scholarly in the group, asked with his head thrust forward in eagerness.

"It is likely that after Christ's time, the priests, monks, and friars turned little by little toward worldly things, and as their customs changed, so their observation of God's laws became different from what Christ bade His priests do. But Poor Priests must proclaim the gospel without desire of gain."

The students asked many questions, and Sir John had ready answers.

"Let the Poor Priests move from place to place. Let them enjoy temporal gifts in moderation, but they are not to have any benefices from prelates of the church."

Someone asked why.

"Because they cannot get a benefice without simony."

Arnold learned how Simon Magus, a sorcerer, converted to Christianity, had offered money to purchase the power of giving the Holy Ghost, and was severely rebuked by Peter.

"God's Word must be taught before all else," Wycliffe emphasized. "It is the bread of life, the seed of regeneration and conversion. More good fruit comes out of preaching God's Word than of any other work."

"Shouldn't we pray?"

"Praying is good," Wycliffe said, "but not so good as preaching. Jesus Christ occupied Himself most in the work of preaching and last in other works."

Several asked how the Word should be preached.

"By adapting it to the comprehension of the hearer. The end of each sermon should be devotion and saving of the soul. Christ promised to His disciples that it should be given to them what to say. The how would follow, but," he added, "in the humble and homely proclamation of the gospel, a flowery style is of little value compared to right substance."

For the first time in the meeting, one of the newcomers ventured a criticism. "Lay people don't have the intellect to understand, do they?"

"Divine illumination alone is needed to interpret the gospel," Wycliffe answered.

"One part of Scripture contradicts the other," a senior student of theology complained.

"Don't tear the Scriptures in pieces as the heretics do. Take them as a whole. Often one part of Scripture explains the other."

"But how can a layman understand Scripture," the newcomer persisted.

"The Holy Ghost teaches us its meaning, just as Christ opened the Scripture to the apostles."

"Lay people don't know Latin."

Wycliffe was patient. "The Bible is our only ground for belief in Christ. Christ and His apostles taught the people in that tongue that was best known to them. Why should men not do so now?"

The training of the Poor Priests continued. The Vice-Chancellor was thrown into prison. The Pope died. There was no more action against Wycliffe. Soon the russet robes at the tailor shop were bought and others ordered for Poor Priests eager to take the gospel story to the lay people of England. They preached in marketplaces, in fields, on streets, two by two, asking for no favor but accepting what people offered.

Arnold and Timothy listened to the stories the Poor Priests told.

"You'll have to take a degree," Timothy announced. "I heard Sir John say a degree taken at Oxford or Cambridge makes God's Word more acceptable. People believe more completely when they hear the Word said by a master."

Arnold grinned. "Do I understand that you are going to be a Poor Priest when you get your degree?"

"Of course." Timothy was unperturbed. "And you should go with me."

"How?" Arnold knew with Father a freeman and working as a tailor, there was more possibility of his entering a college, but he had been so busy helping Dame Margot and listening to Sir John at every opportunity he had almost forgotten about actually taking courses.

"I'll tutor you," Timothy said, his voice casual.

Arnold agreed, first because Timothy had made this offer, and second, because he wanted to learn all he could to be of help to Sir John.

Then Timothy sprang a surprise. Queen's college had provisions for boys without money. With Sir Malcolm's good word and John Wycliffe's backing, Timothy was sure Arnold would be admitted. To Arnold's delight, he was accepted. The college paid for a Latin grammar, a knife, and — to everyone's teasing — a new gown. When Arnold received his haircut — the clerk's tonsure — he felt as if the whole country recognized him as an Oxford student.

At a meeting of the Poor Priests, Arnold felt as if he belonged, even though there were years of study ahead of him.

Someone commented that many lords supported the Poor Priests' teaching.

"That's because they have been to school and have read the works of schoolmen and scholars and can recognize the truth," another student explained.

"We've been talking about people *hearing* the Word of God all the time, and the Poor Priests have been *telling* people parts of the Bible in the English language, but why not let the people read the whole Bible for themselves — in English?"

No one knew afterward just who had made the suggestion. The question had hung in the air over everyone's head, it seemed like to Arnold. The idea was so startling, yet so simple once it was said, why hadn't the idea occurred to anyone before?

"The *whole* Bible?" Wycliffe himself appeared stunned by the idea. He put his hand to his beard, and his eyes gleamed with a faraway look.

The room was silent for several moments.

"When Christ said in the gospel that both heaven and earth should pass but His words would not pass, that is what He meant," Wycliffe's voice rang with a strange new force. "God's Word has passed from Hebrew to Greek, from Greek to Latin, and from Latin to one language after another. Englishmen shall read His Word in English!"

Students leaped to their feet, cheering, clapping each other on the back. The astonishing revelation of their mission was clear to all the people in the room.

The Accusation 10

The translation of the Bible began. John Wycliffe's students, led by Nicholas Hereford and John Purvey, used the Latin Vulgate, since Wycliffe, in spite of his many years of study, had not mastered Greek or Hebrew.

"It's long, slow work," Arnold explained to Lucy on a visit.

"Teach me to read and write," she begged, her eyes gleaming with a secret intent.

"Girls aren't supposed to read and write."

"What would John Wycliffe say to that?"

Arnold opened his mouth to argue, but there was nothing he could say. He knew very well that Wycliffe wanted women to read Scripture, too.

Lucy's quickness at learning amazed Arnold. She practiced every spare minute she could find, and was always ready with her lesson when Arnold and Timothy, too, came to teach her.

"Do you think I'll be able to read the Bible by the time it is translated?" she asked many times in the following months.

Timothy laughed. "You'll know long before at the rate you are learning. There are many problems in translating." He and Arnold were at Dame Margot's giving Lucy a lesson in reading and writing.

"What kind of problems? If a word means something in Latin, all you have to do is put it in English. From what you tell me, the Bible is made of many books, and it will take a long time, but what is so hard about it? If I knew Latin, I could do it, too." Her cocksureness, like a pert little bird, made both boys laugh.

On the next visit, Arnold showed her the problem in translating. He brought a passage from 1 Samuel, second chapter, verse 10: *Dominum formidabunt adversarii ejus* and explained its meaning.

" 'The Lord shall dread the adversaries of him,' " Lucy repeated. "That doesn't make sense. Why should the Lord dread anybody?"

Arnold was triumphant. "That's what I meant about translating. It's long, slow work, and as Timothy told you, there are problems. It isn't enough to translate the words. You have to make sense."

Lucy studied the words again. "It really means 'Adversaries of the Lord shall dread — or, rather, fear — him.' "

The boys stared at each other. For a girl, Lucy was really sharp!

On their way back to the college hall, where Arnold now roomed with Timothy, Arnold mused, "Now I know what Sir John meant when he said, 'No man understands Scripture unless enlightened by the Holy Ghost.' "

"He said it another way, too," Timothy put in. " 'The Holy Ghost always moves some men to study the Bible and understand it.' "

"And women, too, don't forget," Arnold added with a grin.

When Wycliffe's students met in his room to discuss their translations, someone was sure to mention "the Lord's adversaries." The quotation — or misquotation — became a standing joke. Wycliffe admitted the danger of such mistakes was great.

"Well I know what faults there may be from untrue translating," he told them. "There may well be many faults in turning the Scripture from Hebrew into Greek, and from Greek into Latin, and from one language to another. But when such mistakes are found, they must be corrected."

Some tried to argue that since English nobility had copies of the Bible in French, the language of culture, there was no need for a Bible in English.

"This is no longer enough," Wycliffe declared. "Many who read know only English. By using the language of common people, God's law shall be better known." He added, "The worthy kingdom of France, notwithstanding all kinds of difficulties, has translated the Bible from Latin into French. Why shouldn't Englishmen do so too? It is true that the lords of England have the Bible in French, but it is not against reason that they should have it in English, for God's law is for everyone."

Someone mentioned the paternoster, and Wycliffe expounded still more. "Friars have taught in England the paternoster in the English tongue. Since the paternoster is part of Matthew's Gospel, as clerks know, why may not all the gospel be turned into English?" He clinched his argument in his powerful way: "Christ and His apostles taught the people in the tongue most known to them. Should not men do so now? St. Jerome translated the Bible from different languages into Latin so that it might afterward be translated to other tongues."

"But the lay people — they shouldn't have Scripture," someone argued. "That would be heresy, and you have been tried once for your views. Do you think the Pope and the prelates will give up accusing you?"

Wycliffe lost his patience. "What is more heretical than the belief that the laity need not know God's law, that they should content themselves with knowledge imparted orally by the clergy? On the contrary, Holy Scripture is the true faith. The more widely it is known, the better. Laymen must study it firsthand in the language they most readily comprehend."

One of the critics brought up a last argument. "What grievous mistakes the laity will make in reading Scripture."

"Alas, what cruelty is this," Wycliffe responded, "to rob a whole kingdom of bodily food because a few fools may be gluttons, or if a child fail in his lesson at the first day, to suffer no other children to come to lessons because of this default." His voice rose. "What antichrist is this who dares hinder the laity from learning the holy lessons strongly commanded by God?"

Antichrist was a strong word, and the objections now died away.

Two students started an argument on a different matter.

"The word should be *debts*."

"No, it should be *sins*."

The first student translator appealed to the group. "In the Lord's Prayer, which of the words is correct?

Or," he added hopefully, "maybe both should be in it for clarity."

"Read it, read it," someone suggested.

The student complied. "Our Father that art in heaven, hallowed be thy name. Thy realm or kingdom come to thee. Be thy will done on earth as it is done in heaven. Give us today our each day's bread and forgive to us our debts, that is, our sins, as we forgive our debtors, that is to men that have sinned against us, and lead us not into temptation, but deliver us from evil. Amen. So be it."

Wycliffe listened to the reading with a slight frown. "The form and language must be plain and simple." He objected to the use of both words, *debt* and *sin*. "If the soul is not in tune with the words, how can the words have power? Ornamental style is little in keeping with God's Word. The latter is corrupted, its power paralyzed for the conversion of souls. God's Word in its very simplicity has incomparable eloquence."

Another discussion, with some students arguing for one word and others for another word, came up about the biblical command "Thou shalt love the Lord thy God with all thy heart, with all thy life, with all thy thoughts, and with all thy — " Here some claimed the word *strength* was best and others said the word *might* was the right one.

In this way the translation of the Bible — the Gospel first — from Latin into English went on. Weeks went by. At one of her lessons. Lucy had a bit of news for Arnold and Timothy.

"Someone stole one russet robe out of the tailor's shop," she announced. "The tailor and Arnold's father were busy measuring a customer, and when they looked up, a young man was running out the door with this robe draped over his arm."

"At least no one tried to burn the shop," the tailor told them later.

At Blackhall, Arnold and Timothy heard another bit of information.

"Some of the translated pages have been stolen!"

At once, Wycliffe's student associates searched high and low, upstairs and down.

"How many?"

"About a hand-high pile," one of the students said.

When the students heard about the stolen robe, there were many conjectures. "Maybe someone is going alone to preach."

"Starting out with a *stolen* robe?"

"Where is Sir John? He must hear of this — if you are sure the pages of translation have been stolen," Nicholas Hereford said.

"Sir John is not here. He usually takes a walk this time of day," Purvey reminded Nicholas Hereford.

Was this persecution? Were there still spies seeking to find damaging actions Wycliffe was doing? Arnold tried to figure out the answers. The letter that he and Timothy had not been able to recover still rankled in his mind. This time he determined to find out the mystery behind the stolen robe and the stolen translations.

"Some person is doing this," he told Timothy. "It isn't the wind. That person has to be walking around somewhere. If it is a student, he has to eat and sleep."

Timothy understood what Arnold was trying to say. "Yes, and he must talk to somebody. If we keep our eyes and ears open, we ought to be able to overhear *something*."

Timothy paid for their dinner at Blackhall that evening, but Arnold asked if he could act as a serving boy. Timothy explained to the steward, who turned out to be sympathetic. He allowed Arnold to stand with the other servers, a serving cloth over his arm.

Arnold noticed one student sat in the corner. "Why is he eating there?" he whispered to one of the servers.

"He talked in English, instead of Latin."

Six or seven fellows of the college sat with the provost on three sides of a high table, their backs against the wainscoting. Arnold wondered why.

"It's in memory of the Last Supper."

"Or rather," another server said, "once a fellow was stabbed in the back there."

A monk read from a holy book, and the fellows ate in silence.

"I'll never learn anything this way," Arnold told himself. Then a sudden thought came to him. Why not go upstairs and search the rooms while the students ate?

He ran upstairs and opened the doors to each room. A simple table, bookshelf, chair, and bed were all he could find in room after room. The last one was completely empty. The walls were bare. The floor was not even covered with rushes. All that was there was a cushion on the floor, where it had probably dropped from a chair being carried out, and a bed in the corner.

Disappointed, and with growing irritation, Arnold kicked the cushion, feeling instant shame. Wycliffe had a temper too, but he never showed it this way. His temper was aroused only when people tried to hinder God's Word from reaching those who yearned for it.

But the cushion rustled in an odd way when it fell back to the floor. Arnold felt it. Paper rustled under his hand. He pulled out some stitches and drew out the papers. Yes, they were the translations Wycliffe's students had worked so hard on.

He heard footsteps on the stairway. What was he going to do with the pillow now? He decided to simply walk out of the room with the pillow under his arm. His heart thudded so fast he thought it would jump out ahead of him.

"Yes, tonight is my last night," he heard an older students tell someone. "I have to go to London tomorrow."

The voice sounded familiar, but Arnold could not place it. He walked as calmly as he could to the head of the stairs.

"Stop! That's my pillow you're taking!" The older student snatched the pillow and shoved Arnold so hard he had to catch himself on the wooden railing to prevent himself from falling down the stairs.

Arnold expected the student to come after him, to arrest him, but nothing happened. When he told Timothy later, Timothy was puzzled, too.

"Leaving for London? Why would he leave right in the middle of the term? Was he expelled again?"

Neither boy could answer the questions. Arnold was still puzzling about the student a week later when he went to give Lucy a reading lesson.

When Arnold kicked the cushion it rustled in an odd way
as it fell back to the floor.

"First I have to get the key to the rector's garden," she said.

"Key? What for?"

"My mother has washed some shirts, and I'm to lay them out on the grass to dry. Come with me."

The rector stood at his doorway with lips pursed in disapproval. "No, I do not dare let the key out of my hands. Last week you forgot and left the gate open. Two or three students rushed in with lighted torches and burned some papers and an old cushion. They tramped on my young pea vines." The rector's voice rose in indignation. "My young peas were trampled into the dirt, and I do so like a dish of new peas," he added in an aggrieved tone. "You'll have to find some other place to dry the shirts."

Lucy turned away, two bright spots of red on her cheeks. "I know I left the gate open," she admitted, "but a Poor Priest called to me, but it was the strangest thing. When I went over to him, he turned his back. I didn't know what to do, and I forgot all about the key."

Papers? *Cushion*? When Timothy heard about them later at the tailor shop, he was as excited as Arnold and Lucy. Lucy clutched Arnold's arm. "There he is! It must be the same person. There was only one last week, and the Poor Priests go in pairs."

A russet-clad man was walking up the street, his head muffled, his robe reaching to his sandaled feet.

"But he doesn't have a staff."

Arnold, Lucy, and Timothy stared at each other. Arnold read the same question on their faces that he had in his mind. Was this the mysterious spy who had stolen the translations and burned them?

"He mustn't get away," Lucy whispered.

"But how can we stop him if he wants to go?" the boys replied.

"We can grab hold of him and at least find out who he is. It might even be someone we know, or at least we can describe him to Sir John," Lucy argued.

"He always said there was a Judas in every group," Timothy reasoned.

"Maybe more than one."

"Let's rush him," Lucy suggested.

"Take him by surprise," Arnold added.

"I'll flap my apron in his face."

The three timed themselves. "One, two, three — go!"

They rushed forward. Arnold grabbed the man from behind. Timothy clung to his arms, and Lucy flapped her apron, screaming at the top of her voice.

The man turned. His slight figure under their strong grasp almost toppled over.

It was John Wycliffe.

The Intruders 11

Arnold, Timothy, and Lucy burst out with instant apologies and explanations.

"I remember now that you bought a robe," Arnold said.

"But there was only one of you," Lucy began.

"And Poor Priests go by twos," Timothy added.

"And the student who stole the papers and burned them — "

"Was leaving for London — "

"And we thought — "

Wycliffe was embarrassed, too. He admitted he often walked for exercise and sometimes enjoyed wearing the robe of a Poor Priest to feel as if he were going out to bring welcome news of the gospel to people over England.

Then John Purvey ran up, panting. "I hoped I would find you here. We've caught the man who stole the translations. He says he's only following Bishop Courtenay's orders. What do you want done with him?"

"Let him go."

"Let him go?" Purvey echoed. He looked as if he thought John Wycliffe had lost his senses. "But he was wearing a Poor Priest's robe."

"Then he's the one who *stole* the robe," Lucy whispered to the boys. Arnold and Timothy nodded. The mystery of the stolen robe was solved.

"Poor Priests teach God's law to their enemies and pray for them as Christ did on the cross," Wycliffe reminded Purvey.

Two Oxford officials came up with the student between them. "We were directed to find you here," they explained. "What charges do you wish to bring?"

The young man refused to look up or speak. Why did he seem so familiar? Arnold asked himself.

Lucy supplied the answer. "Why, it's the beggar!"

She was right. But how different he looked now as a student! No wonder Arnold hadn't recognized him, clean-shaven, with the shaved circle on top of his head. How different he looked in the rags and matted beard and hair of a beggar!

"Let him go," Wycliffe instructed the officers.

"But Sir John, he was the one who led a student revolt against you," Purvey argued.

Nevertheless, the young man was released. He seemed neither pleased nor displeased. "Bishop Courtenay would have set me free anyway," he announced on leaving.

"Then he really was a spy for Bishop Courtenay!" Lucy exclaimed.

"Not only that," Timothy told Arnold and Lucy later, "it was Bishop Courtenay who ordered the chancellor to let him come back to Queen's College."

Later, at Dame Margot's, Arnold, Timothy, and Lucy went over all the details of the beggar and the strange way he had become part of the story of Wycliffe's work.

"Is it true you have to kneel before the fellows of the college at meals?" Lucy asked in an abrupt change of subject.

"No. I sit with Timothy. I don't kneel. Why?" Arnold asked.

"I heard that poor scholars have to kneel."

Timothy flushed and tried to talk about something else, but Arnold insisted on knowing more. It turned out that Timothy had been paying for Arnold's meals, and that as a poor boy of the college Arnold should be kneeling before the fellows of the hall and eating their scraps.

"Then I want to do what the poor boys do," Arnold declared.

"But I know how you feel about kneeling before another," Timothy said, even more embarrassed.

Arnold remembered that long ago he had hated the idea of subjecting himself to the commands of another. Now he laughed. "I want to do it."

Timothy looked doubtful. "But you will have to eat the leavings of the others. It's like begging, and you always hated that."

"Good training for being a Poor Priest," Arnold said.

"Let's both transfer to Blackhall," Timothy suggested. "I've heard they don't have enough senior students and they're renting out rooms. Besides, we'll be closer to Sir John."

The transfer was made, and Arnold cheerfully knelt while others ate and took their leavings as his food. To be going to college and to be near John Wycliffe mattered far more than the token submission he was required to do as a poor boy.

In the lecture hall, behind the pulpit, and in his writings, John Wycliffe was pouring forth his pleas for men of the church to return to Christ's teachings, using the Bible as their source of inspiration, rather than the Pope's declarations or the interpretations by high-ranking prelates. His working days grew longer and longer.

Always slight of figure, Wycliffe grew even more slight.

"Weak body, fiery soul," a student remarked in admiration.

"I heard that even one of his enemies called him 'the flower of Oxford,'" another said.

Friars of the four different orders visited him. Sometimes Arnold and Timothy listened to their disputes in the lower hall.

"This preaching of Scripture must stop," a friar insisted.

"To prohibit preaching is to prevent the influence of the Spirit," Wycliffe retorted.

"Your Poor Preachers are only another order," another friar accused him.

"Not so," Wycliffe answered. "The Poor Preachers take no vows whatever. Where an order makes a rule to rise at midnight, such rising may sometimes do good but often it does evil. To have rules and vows without God is the presumption of Satan. Therefore, men will acknowledge Holy Writ and the living of Christ for their rule, and will study the Bible because it is the whole truth."

"Why do you quote the learned doctors so much?" still another friar sneered on a visit to Blackhall.

Arnold and Timothy joined other students who clustered on the stairway to hear Wycliffe dispute with the friars.

"No created being has the power to reverse the

sense of Christian faith," Wycliffe responded. "The holy doctors put us in no difficulty but rather teach us to abstain from the love of novelties. What Christ taught us is enough for this life. Go to the Holy Book for authority, not the hierarchy of the church fathers."

"Just what do you have against the friars — you who had so many friends among them once?"

At this question, Wycliffe's shriveled body tensed. "Friars profess poverty but they are untrue to the rule. They sell indulgences, absolutions, pardons, special prayers."

"You should remember that a friar from each of the four orders defended you at the trial at St. Paul's."

Wycliffe retorted, "We know well that the devil often does much good."

"But you know it is heresy to put holy things before dogs, and your translating Scripture is just one of many heresies you have committed."

"Christ commanded that men should not give holy things to dogs or put precious pearls before hogs. He also said not to speak God's Word where there is no one to hear. But now it has come to pass that if a God-fearing priest lives a good life in meekness and in giving alms to poor men, and not wasting poor men's tithes in vain feasts or ornaments, but holding himself in devoutness and in teaching God's law in truth and from Holy Writ, he is held to be a niggard, a dog, or a hog, a hypocrite, and a heretic."

No matter how the friars complained, Wycliffe had an answer. When one accused his answers as being defective in substance and form, Wycliffe replied with his usual swiftness. "That is not the way to untie knots, for so might a magpie contradict all and every proof." He added, "Oh, if the apostles could hear this subtle hairsplitting, how much they would despise it."

"He knows by heart the most abstruse parts of Aristotle," one of the students in Blackhall said later.

Both Arnold and Timothy could see tension mounting. Instead of mischievous college students rioting against Wycliffe, the friars themselves were aroused. In the lecture hall, the boys heard Wycliffe speak about transubstantiation. His view shocked many students in training to become priests.

"What!" one demanded, leaping to his feet. "Do you deny Christ's presence in the host?"

"Anyone can see the host is bread," Wycliffe retorted. "The very mice know it for such."

"But Sir John, if the bread remains bread and the body of Christ remains in heaven, what does happen?"

"Christ is present spiritually."

Although this answer seemed reasonable to Arnold and Timothy, others eagerly quoted the latest view of Wycliffe. Soon it reached London, and John of Gaunt hurried to Oxford. Tall, spare, and erect, he pleaded with Wycliffe not to press the idea.

"Sometimes it harms men to tell the truth at an improper time, and it always harms one to lie," Wycliffe admitted, "and I know that Christ and His apostles waited for the right time to speak, but I cannot now keep still."

John of Gaunt shook his head and left.

"The end of his protection," students whispered among themselves. "Sir John should not express his views so strongly."

But John Wycliffe continued his writing, teaching, and preaching until he became ill.

There were more whispers. "Wycliffe is in disfavor with the king's government and the church. He must face the consequence of his views. Who will help him now?"

Students in Blackhall tiptoed past Wycliffe's sickroom. Their talk was subdued. "He's a dying man," the whispers ran. "He'll be dead within this seven-night."

Timothy hired a horse and a servant and went to London to see if his father, Sir Malcolm, could find a doctor who could save Wycliffe.

Arnold helped Purvey take care of the desperately ill man. Downstairs to the kitchen, up again to Wycliffe's room, Arnold brought soups and porridge in the hope of getting Wycliffe to eat. Each time he came upstairs, he wondered if Wycliffe had died.

The porter said visitors were outside waiting to see Wycliffe.

"Visitors?" Arnold heard Purvey exclaim. "Impossible. The man is on his deathbed. There will be no visitors."

"But these are the friars — one from each order," the porter explained.

Purvey threw his hands up. "They are the last who will get to see Sir John."

"But they are not alone. Four aldermen of Oxford are with them."

Purvey ground his teeth. "Do they insist on seeing a dead man?" He bounded up the stairs. "You and the other students hold them off," he told Arnold, who clung to the rail, uncertain whether to go upstairs or down.

The porter admitted the visitors to the entrance hall.

"Wasn't that John Purvey who spoke to us?" one asked.

"Yes. John Wycliffe's amanuensis."

"Is it his translation or Wycliffe's, would you say?" a friar asked.

The others shrugged. "It's all the same. Heresy is heresy, wherever you find it, but Wycliffe must be held accountable first."

For a while, the visitors made no move to ascend. Then, as if of one mind, they mounted the stairway. When Arnold saw that they were in earnest, he pushed past the other students and hurried to Wycliffe's room.

"They're coming," he told Purvey.

"Bolt the door, then. We won't let them in."

A moan from the sickbed sent Purvey scurrying to Wycliffe's side. Arnold saw the sunken cheeks, the hawklike nose, and the sensitive lips of the gospel doctor. *Is he already dead?* he asked himself.

A voice thundered outside the sickroom. "Hola within! We come in the name of the church."

"There is a dying man here. He can see no one," Purvey called out, at the same time pulling the curtains of the bed closed.

"We represent the church. He must see us to gain absolution."

"He needs no absolution. He's in the hands of God now," Purvey retorted.

From behind the curtains of the sickbed, Wycliffe gasped, "Wait! Who wants to see me?"

"Tell him," Purvey hissed to Arnold. "I'll stand by the door."

"Four friars, Sir John," Arnold said. "One from each order."

"Four — friars." Wycliffe sounded like he laughed.

"And four aldermen, too, sir, from Oxford."

"I — cannot — see — them like this. Purvey — where are my clothes?" Wycliffe sounded stronger.

"But, Sir John —"

"My clothes, my clothes, an' it please you."

Purvey pulled the curtains apart. "Your academic robe, Sir John?"

"No, my russet. Yes, my russet robe."

Purvey brought out a clean shirt, hose, tunic, doublet, and the russet robe. He had Arnold spread a sheet over a chair, with a foot sheet on the floor.

"No — no. Just dress me in bed."

When Wycliffe was dressed, he gasped. "Let them come in."

The four friars entered first, followed by the four aldermen. They arranged themselves in two rows facing Wycliffe.

"Good health," a friar intoned. "May God grant you a speedy recovery." The others coughed and echoed the wish.

Wycliffe's eyes, unnaturally bright, flashed open, then closed. He clasped his hands on the outside of his coverlet. His fingers looked brittle and as white as tally sticks.

A friar cleared his throat and leaned forward. "But since we know that you are on the point of death — "

Wycliffe's eyelids fluttered.

"We ask for a retraction of what you have said against us."

Wycliffe stirred, but Arnold could see he was too weak to raise himself in bed.

Another friar took over. "You have dealt us heavy blows in word and writing. Now, in your last moments, in the presence of these worthy aldermen, who will attest what you say, show your penitence by formally withdrawing your charges against the four orders."

Wycliffe did not stir.

"We are too late." Disappointment colored the friar's voice. He turned to the others. "Good sirs, we are talking to a dead man."

After Purvey raised him up on his pillows, Wycliffe cried out with eyes flashing, "I shall not die but I shall live and declare the works of the Lord."

God's Word Triumphant

12

The four friars and the four aldermen let out a groan of disappointment.

"May his soul burn in hell for eternity," a friar intoned.

At these words, Wycliffe's emaciated frame shook as if with palsy. His lusterless eyes gleamed like fire.

"Raise me on my pillows," he ordered Purvey, and then cried out, "I shall not die but I shall live and declare the works of the Lord."

A strength, power, and radiance shot forth from Wycliffe's wasted body and filled the room. The visitors, stunned and awed by the sight of a man rising on his deathbed, turned and all but ran out.

By the time Timothy arrived from London with the special doctor Sir Malcolm had sent, Wycliffe was well enough to start his writing, teaching, and preaching with renewed strength. His recovery was the marvel of Oxford.

There were many versions of what had actually been said when John Wycliffe rose from his deathbed.

"I know it for a fact," the brother-in-law of an alderman said. "Wycliffe rose straight up on his pillows without any help and said, 'I shall not die but live and declare the works of the Lord.'"

Another insisted that Wycliffe's words were: "I shall live and declare the church triumphant."

In his own heart, Arnold knew what Wycliffe had said and why. The evils of the church had to be attacked first so that God's Word could triumph. God had given John Wycliffe a temper to use as a tool for His work.

"Sir John was so angry he couldn't die," Arnold told Timothy and Lucy.

Wycliffe himself said of his recovery, "Every natural body is given power from God to resist what is hostile to it, and of duly preserving itself."

But it was not just to preserve his own body that Wycliffe recovered.

"When we pray the Lord's Prayer, we ask God to give us our each day's bread," Wycliffe explained, "and it should be made our bread by our true service to Him."

At Dame Margot's, Arnold enthusiastically explained a new understanding that had come to him. "To serve — that's the key."

Lucy laughed. "I've already found that out."

"How?" Arnold asked, a little annoyed that Lucy was ahead of him again.

Lucy explained how she was serving. She had been teaching her mother, Arnold's parents, and the tailor how to read and write. The little group met regularly.

"When will the Bible be ready?" she asked.

Both Arnold and Timothy tried to explain how long it took even after the translation was made to write out other copies.

"We'll be ready to read it," she promised.

The boys in turn promised to help the little group learn to write and read. Their eagerness gave Arnold a sudden glimpse into the future.

Someday, everyone would be able to read!

But Wycliffe's enemies had not been silenced.

"His false teachings must be stopped," they said, and refused to listen to his answer: "If Holy Writ be false, then God, the Author, is false."

Others puzzled over Wycliffe's unusual ideas.

"They're heresies! They're — they're unspeakable! Why, he says Christ is the lowest creature because he is the first matter."

Still others raged, "If you plead with him to tell the truth, he says, 'Get behind me, Satan, for thou art not knowledgeable in the truth of God.'"

"Or," one said indignantly, "he says, 'Truth is nothing else but God's thought.'"

Wycliffe's students pleaded, "Can't you be less outspoken?" They explained the church as a whole was preparing to silence him.

"I say with Paul, 'Woe is unto me, if I preach not,'" was Wycliffe's reply. "It is antichrist who says that the preaching of the gospel makes dissension and enmity. Antichrist would quench and outlaw Holy Writ and thus make all men damned, but truly, if any man preaches in grace, there comes more good than the harm done by all the fiends together. Thousands of Satan's children are deeper damned for their revolt against God and His gracious teachings."

By this time almost everyone in Oxford must have known about the translation of the Bible.

"Who is to read it?" the friars and monks of the four orders sneered. "The beggars in the street?"

Timothy's father came down from London to warn Wycliffe that his enemies were past the talking stage. The king himself was writing letters commanding that a stop be put to Wycliffe's heretical opinions.

"The sheriff and the mayor of Oxford have been ordered to help put this decree into effect," Sir Malcolm said.

"Do you think they can stop God's law from taking effect?" Wycliffe asked.

Sir Malcolm sighed. "What must be, will be." He left for London, with parting advice to Arnold and Timothy. "Stand by Sir John. If ever he needed his friends, it is now." He added, "If only Sir John had taken John of Gaunt's advice, he would not now be in disfavor, but we can do no more. God's will be done."

Soon afterward, twelve doctors, plus six friars, four seculars, and two monks, were appointed to report on Wycliffe's teachings.

"But only the barest majority reported against me," Wycliffe said when the report had been made.

Wycliffe's friends shook their heads. "This is no real victory."

Everyone waited for the next step. Day by day the tension grew. Students stared at one another in passing. Who was friend and who was foe of the heretical John Wycliffe? If an official of Oxford stepped inside Blackhall, the place became deserted in a few moments. Rumors flew. "They're going to throw him in chains and take him to London." "He will have to answer charges at Canterbury in secret." "The Pope himself is going to make him come to Rome."

Arnold and Timothy returned to Blackhall one day after a visit to the little group at Dame Margot's. The minute they stepped inside the hall, Arnold knew something decisive had happened. Students ran shouting from one room to another.

"Search the hall!"

"What for?"

"The sayings of John Wycliffe."

"Who said?"

"The Chancellor."

Arnold and Timothy learned that Wycliffe's writings had already been spirited away by friends who were in the hall when the order came.

"Search the hall!" The cry came again. "Seize all those who maintain heretical opinions!"

"Seize all those who have books by John Wycliffe."

Timothy drew Arnold to one side. "I have a sermon of his that I've been reading."

"Get it — hide it," Arnold implored. "We'll take it to the tailor shop." He waited in nervous suspense until Timothy came downstairs, walking slowly and with head high. But someone must have seen the writing.

"There's one of them!"

Several students jumped on Timothy, and when Arnold went to his defense, they seized Arnold, too.

"To the river!"

A group of students surrounded Arnold, Timothy, and several others of Wycliffe's friends, hustled them to the river, and while the sheriff and mayor of Oxford stood by, threw them into the water. Arnold sputtered and got to his feet in time to see the students stream back across the field toward the hall, looking for other victims.

Timothy wrung out his clothes and said, "Is that all they can do?"

That evening at dinner, the Chancellor made an announcement. "Good sirs, Oxford is the seat of learning. There are many doctors here capable of conducting students through to their baccalaureate, masters' and doctors' degrees. Sometimes it is necessary for a teacher to withdraw, or for some other reason be unable to fulfill a teaching commitment."

Arnold heard an implied threat in the Chancellor's voice. What was coming next?

"Some of you may have to change classes because of just such a situation." The Chancellor coughed, looked down at his wooden trencher, and waited until the slight rustle had subsided. "John Wycliffe will no longer be lecturing at Oxford."

In spite of the rule of silence at meals, the room filled with murmurs.

Later, in his room, John Wycliffe had little to say. Purvey had packed Wycliffe's books and papers, and had already hired a cart and horse.

"But where will you go? What will you do?" Wycliffe's friends asked.

"I'll go to Lutterworth, of course. There is much to do — my sermons and finishing the translation." Then he prayed. "Oh, Jesus Christ, stop these blasphemies of antichrist. Make Thy holy gospel known and kept by Thy simple brethren. Increase in them faith, hope, and charity. Soften, O marvelous power of the Divine Seed, the hearts hard as stone."

When he left Oxford, Wycliffe looked back once. "The house of God and the gate of heaven," he told his friends. A tear gleamed in his eye, but he did not look back after that.

After Wycliffe's withdrawal from Oxford, Arnold and Timothy visited him many times at Lutterworth. Both boys were ready to go out as Poor Priests whenever Wycliffe gave the word. Laymen had already been sent out successfully.

"An unlettered man with God's grace can do more for building up the church than many graduates," Wycliffe admitted, "because the former scatters the seed of the law of Christ more humbly and more abundantly both in deed and in word."

At one time he had argued on the other side. "The apostles took no such degree," he said now, and noted that some men received the cap of the master's degree through their gifts of many hundred pounds. "Wax doctors," he said in scorn of the letters sealed in wax by lords who commanded the colleges to give the gift-givers such degrees. "They run from hard study like wax from fire."

Going out too soon as a Poor Priest would be running away from studies, too, Arnold decided. "Besides," he told Timothy, "I'll never forget what it is like to be poor. The people we will reach will recognize me for what I am, and our cause will be all the stronger because you will be giving up material possessions and a tithe for God."

Their eagerness was whetted by the completion of the New Testament, with the Old Testament soon to follow, in the language of the Englishman. At the same time, Parliament passed a bill for sheriffs to imprison preachers of heresy, but the House of Commons rejected it. It was plain, however, that the controversy would not cease..

"Do we have enough faith?" he asked Timothy, and was embarrassed when Timothy put the question to Wycliffe.

"Faith is like a lens," John Wycliffe said. "Properly arranged, it will enable us to see things far off as if near, and," he added with a smile, "to read minute letters like young men."

Arnold knew without a doubt that someday he and Timothy would be on the roads and byways of England as beggars without openly begging. With the Scripture in hand and faith in their hearts, neither mockery nor threat would prevent the Beggars' Bible from reaching the faithful in heart.

As Wycliffe said, "Who knows the measure of God's mercy to whom hearing of God's Word shall thus profit? No man shall be saved but he that willfully hears and endlessly keeps God's law."

NOTE: John Wycliffe died December 31, 1384. In spite of all the action taken against him, he had never been excommunicated; therefore, he was buried on consecrated ground. In 1428, his bones were torn from the grave in Lutterworth churchyard by the English bishop at the command of the Pope, burned to ashes, thrown into the river Swift, and from there they were carried from brook to river, river to ocean. The seeds of his doctrine sprang up in every land.

Are These Words New to You?

Abbot: A man in charge of men who live a religious life away from the world.

Amanuensis: A person who copies down what another says, or who copies something written.

Beadle: A policeman.

Bondman: A person one step higher than a slave.

Donatio: A gift to the church.

Fosse: A ditch.

Friar: A man who travels around begging money, eggs, grain, etc., for the church.

Garth: An enclosed garden.

Habit: The clothes worn by men who withdraw from the world for religious reasons.

Lap dog: Any pet dog small enough to be held in the lap.

Mendicant Orders: Groups of men who beg money, goods, crops, for the church.

Monastery: A building where religious men live.

Monk: A man who withdraws from the world and lives in self-denial for religious reasons.

Paternoster: The Lord's Prayer. (*Pater* means father; *noster* means our.)

Prelate: A high-ranking man of the church.

Rector: A minister or preacher.

Reeve: A man who oversees a large household or estate. He collects taxes from people who rent land from the owner.

Serf: A person who is bound to his master's land and is transferred with it to a new owner.

Tankard: A large drinking cup with handle.

Trencher: A wooden plate.

Writ: A legal paper setting forth a law.

THE AUTHOR

Louise A. Vernon was born in Coquille, Oregon. Her grandparents crossed the plains in covered wagons as young children.

She earned her BA degree from Willamette University, Salem, Oregon, and studied music at Cincinnati Conservatory. She took advanced studies in music in Los Angeles, after which she turned to Christian journalism. Following three years of special study in creative writing, she began her successful series of religious-heritage juveniles. She teaches creative writing in the San Jose public school district.

Mrs. Vernon re-creates for children the stories of Reformation times and acquaints them with great figures in church history. She has traveled throughout England and Germany researching firsthand the settings for her stories. In each book she places a child on the scene with the historical character and involves him in an exciting plot.

The National Association of Christian Schools, representing more then 8,000 Christian educators, honored *Ink on His Fingers* as one of the two best children's books with a Christian message released in 1972.

Mrs. Vernon is author of *Peter and the Pilgrims* (early America), *Strangers in the Land* (the Huguenots), *The Secret Church* (the Anabaptists), *The Bible Smuggler* (William Tyndale), *Key to the Prison* (George Fox and the Quakers), *Night Preacher* (Menno Simons and the Anabaptists), *The Beggars' Bible* (John Wycliffe), *Ink on His Fingers* (Johann Gutenberg), *Doctor in Rags* (Paracelsus and the Hutterites), *Thunderstorm in Church* (Martin Luther), *A Heart Strangely Warmed* (John Wesley), *The Man Who Laid the Egg* (Erasmus), and *The King's Book* (the King James version of the Bible).